DUST TO DUST

Where fiction meets reality

PIERCE KNIGHT

Dust to Dust
Copyright © 2017 by Pierce Knight

All rights reserved. No part of this publication may be reproduced, distributed, or transmitted in any form or by any means, including photocopying, recording, or other electronic or mechanical methods, without the prior written permission of the author, except in the case of brief quotations embodied in critical reviews and certain other non-commercial uses permitted by copyright law.

Tellwell Talent
www.tellwell.ca

ISBN
978-1-77302-164-5 (Paperback)
978-1-77302-165-2 (eBook)

Dedicated to someone special I love, whom I offended many years ago and for which I am truly sorry

TABLE OF CONTENTS

Prologue vii
Chapter One 1
Chapter Two 10
Chapter Three 17
Chapter Four 25
Chapter Five 33
Chapter Six 40
Chapter Seven 47
Chapter Eight 53
Chapter Nine 60
Chapter Ten 68
Chapter Eleven 77
Chapter Twelve 84
Chapter Thirteen 92
Chapter Fourteen 99
Chapter Fifteen 109
Chapter Sixteen 115
Chapter Seventeen 122
Chapter Eighteen 128
Chapter Nineteen 140
Chapter Twenty 147
Chapter Twenty One 155
Epilogue 163

PROLOGUE

THE SHRILL SCREAM OF VENGEANCE WAS ABOUT to pierce the star- studded night and rob it of tranquility. The conscience of the living dead was awakened to a fiery blast of reality. Loudspeakers were blaring atop every minaret and steeple. This city of a thousand mosques and churches, ravaged by centuries of inequity and corruption emerged from its dark past, its lifeblood energized by the universal message of hope that now reverberated from every corner. A saviour had arrived.

A new dawn heralded the advent of the Messenger of the Covenant. He sat there like a refiner scooping away the foamy froth and leaving the precious metal behind to quench the thirst of the faithful.

Desperate with pangs of hunger, the lonely werewolf hunted its prey in the pitch of the dark, moonless night to devour the souls of the faithful. The trees were petrified into silence by sheer trepidation in the still of the eerie night. Not an animal dared to move even in the slightest. Like sheep they lay down in total capitulation, felled by the werewolf's ghastly spell. Yet the bravest of them made an undaunted sprint for the Pearly Gates to hear the rehearsal of the ultimate prayer that was being orchestrated.

"My children, Luciano Vargas was the embodiment of all that is wilful, as he bathed in depravity to the accompaniment of broomstick fiddle played by the six bent-knuckled wicked witches, who hopped around in gleeful merriment."

"Go on, Lawrence Forebearer, go on. You must." pleaded the children incessantly. With great reluctance, the storyteller turned over the page to a new leaf, only to reveal the dreaded words 'The End'.

As abruptly as it had begun, the story ended. Just over the horizon lay a new beginning. From the dust of its ashes, the phoenix arose once again, to reach great heights of prominence. The epic battle of good vs evil had just started.

CHAPTER ONE

GABRIEL BOLLINGER WAS AWAKENED BY AN ALL too familiar fluttering noise.

"Jake!" Gabriel exclaimed as he noticed the hoopoe sitting on the railing of the balcony. "My little friend, how are you doing?" Jake fluttered his feathers and danced a few steps closer to where Gabriel was. He had known Gabriel for many years and liked him immensely. "Doing splendid my man."

"So are you ever going to tell me how old you are, Jake?"

The hoopoe answered with the same answer he always did. "A lot younger than you think."

Gabriel wondered why he even bothered asking since he knew the answer, but he hoped that one day Jake would let up and tell him. Jake had a habit of answering with a straight face, but over the years Gabriel had learned to discern the slight smirk around the corners of Jake's lips as he spoke.

"And what are the latest happenings in the Forest of Wonders?"
"Not much, everybody is going around doing their job,"

Jake replied flapping his wings once more as he settled down besides Gabriel.

Seeing that Jake was not giving up much information, Gabriel pressed on. "Is Ronaldo giving everyone a hard time?"

Jake knew Ronaldo the white pawed lion was the king of the jungle. He had been appointed by the Great King to keep an eye on the inhabitants of the Forest of Wonders, just to make sure they were all right and did not get into any trouble. Jake also knew that Ronaldo was a bit moody and a strict disciplinarian and had gotten into a few terse situations with the carefree bird.

"He is his old self but I suppose he is doing just fine."

"Well, do give him my regards, and here let me send him a personal note with good wishes," said Gabriel as he got up, grabbed a pen and paper and wrote something on a slip. Then he rolled the note and secured it to Jake's leg with a pin. "Off you go and don't forget to give this to Ronaldo."

"Ouch, you always do this. You know you could have used string, if you only bothered to get some," said the bird as he flew away into the distant sunset.

As he turned to head indoors, Gabriel noticed a wisp of pink smoke rising in the distance from one of the minarets of the golden domed palace and admired it for a few moments. The smoke was an everyday occurrence yet something that never went unnoticed by Gabriel's attentive eyes.

The smoke signal system was designed mainly as a light show to entertain the public. But it was also used at times to communicate special messages to certain individuals. Pink coloured smoke always rose from the main turret located on the south east corner of the dome. It gave a pleasant sight to the beholder. Frequently there were streaks of green, orange and yellow.

Gabriel was marvelling at the light show as he frequently had and was just turning around once again to go inside when something caught the corner of his eye. Pink wisps of smoke had turned to subtle red streaks. When there were streaks of red as well, it signalled that a matter of great concern had to be addressed, and only a few people knew this.

"Omigosh, the King has an important announcement in the Royal Court. I better get there in a hurry," Gabriel said to himself.

* * * *

A half hour earlier, Gabriel strode across the marble tiled floor of his luxurious penthouse towards the French doors that opened onto the balcony. He stepped into the warmth of the early afternoon sunlight and looked down eighteen floors at the magnificent Central Square of the Great Kingdom. Fourteen tree lined boulevards led to the square at the centre of which was a spectacular water fountain. Embellished with coloured lights at the base, the fountain waters rose some one hundred and fifty feet into the air. Gardens laden with ponds and walkways surrounded the fountain. It was a busy Saturday afternoon and the citizens of the Great Kingdom strolled through the park-like setting or sat along the benches. Some played with Frisbees or watched their children on the swings. Gabriel lifted his gaze towards the south-east and saw the massive golden dome of the palace of the Great King looming in the distant horizon. With a smile on his face he turned around, grabbed a glass of fresh pomegranate juice and lay down on a deck chair. As he closed his eyes and felt the cool sweet juice against his tongue, he stepped down memory lane and could not help smiling.

Life had been very good for Gabriel. Having lived here for many years in the midst of very comfortable furnishings, he had grown accustomed to the niceties of his surroundings. The penthouse had fifteen foot ground to ceiling windows that offered a panoramic view of the Capital City below.

Several landmarks were strewn across the Capital City. Sixteen miles to the east, the glistening Marvel Communications tower, made of granite and covered with special white marble rose upward to a staggering height of 4534 feet making it the tallest structure in the Kingdom. The Distinguished Citizens Hall of Fame, lined with statues of the city's notable who had contributed to the well-being of others, was situated a mile west. And the Museum of Antiquities sat beside the glass domed Museum of Wildlife a short distance from Central Square. It drew upon the rich history and artifacts of the Kingdom to enlighten and endear the visitors with respect for their nation. A very popular shopping destination, the Grand Bazaar of Luxury Goods with its seventy little turrets and covering over 375000 square feet was besides the thirty-two acre, ninety-nine-slide Childrens' Waterpark Complex.

Inside Gabriel's penthouse, the living room offered a cosy place to relax. A sleek cream coloured sectional sofa surrounded by black glass side tables and accented with crimson lamps sat across from a giant seventy-five inch flat screen television. Behind the sofa hung a colourful sixteen by nine foot mural of three hunters making their way through dense forest as they embarked on a foot safari, surrounded by lush vegetation and an assortment of wild animals. The smell of musk permeated the atmosphere of the room and added to the ambience of soft instrumental music resonating against the slightly curved walls. When drawn, a set of heavy burgundy drapes shut the light out immersing the living room into soft amber lighting. When open they let the bright sunshine in and made the hunting mural come to vibrant, colourful life.

"Ten thousand years of peace and prosperity without wars," he muttered to himself. "There is plenty to eat, no one is greedy and everybody gets anything they want. How sweet life feels." Contentment was written all over his face as he sipped on the pomegranate juice.

Incredible advances had been made in stem cell research and DNA repair. Individual genes that influenced lifespan had been isolated and nurtured in the proper environment and combined with the proper diet and caloric intake had greatly boosted the lifespan of the average person. In particular the gene SIR-2, which regulates DNA packaging was administered in the proper dosage. Stems cells were taken from blood and used to repair unhealthy organs resulting in virtually no disease at all. All this led to a population that did not age and seemed to live forever.

Gabriel stood up and reached for some more pomegranate juice from the bottle on the side table next to his chair "Everyone is so happy. What a marvellous system we live in."

The system Gabriel was talking about was instituted by the Great King. It was based on freedom - freedom of travel, freedom of speech and freedom of action. Everyone was responsible for their behaviour rather than blaming others. They raced with one another to be in the forefront of the righteous. Their motto was to treat each other as they would want to be treated, and they persevered very hard in doing this. People used their conscience as a moral compass. Even though they had the freedom to leave, no one wanted to of their own free will. Contentment was the lot of the people, and they led a vibrant, satisfying life without stress. Elimination of stress had led to the extinction of disease. There were plentiful provisions for all, and no one was greedy or jealous.

The Great Kingdom was divided into 14931 zones, with each zone having a mayor. Being a mayor of a zone meant having a high rank and associated bounties but was largely a ceremonial position. The King's Guard did all the work that was necessary. Yet, even they did not have much to do since the system pretty much ran by itself. They mostly distributed provisions from the Great King's treasury. There were no elections. There was no need for them. All decisions were taken at the zone level by a council that reached unanimous consensus. The best person for a job was picked. Best decisions for the people were made based on a scorecard of weighing pros and cons. It was the elimination of greed and ego that allowed unanimous consensus to be such a success. Arguing and deliberations that frequently led to gridlock and indecision did not happen. There was no bickering or dispute.

Every person felt worthwhile. Whatever gender or race a person belonged to, there was no racism whatsoever. Crime was unknown, and there were no prisons. Neither was there promiscuity, unwanted pregnancies, sexually transmitted diseases or single parents. Society enjoyed the benefits of joyous, close knit families surrounded by caring friends. They laughed and joked together and counted their blessings.

A number of very important departments had been set up to efficiently manage the Kingdom. They were all developed by the King and based on a critical technology called Advanced Atomic Control or AAC. This technology could encapsulate all the atoms of a target object and then exercise control over them, moving them to a different location, rearranging them or even putting them in a 'sleep' state. Several applications including weaponry were built on the foundation of AAC. Satellites used AAC for detailed monitoring, laser guns used AAC to target individual atoms and AAC transponders were used to move people from one location to another almost instantly if need be. Given the need, one could aim an AAC transporter towards themselves, adjust the speed, enter the coordinates and fly over to the desired destination.

Furthermore, AAC could be used to prevent earthquakes, calm the seas and clean the atmosphere of harmful toxins. It could also control the thoughts and moods of people. However, this function was disabled on most devices. It could only be activated and used on direct orders of the King and only when it affected national security.

There was the Department of Provisions that calculated and distributed the needs of the populace. It used satellites to monitor the work performance of each individual and precisely deliver the exact reward of provisions on target so that there was absolutely no unfairness. The Department of Public Well-Being could analyze the actions and brain waves and thoughts of individuals to ensure mental happiness. There had not been the need to do that because people were in a euphoric state but the capability existed. Then there was the King's Armoury, operated by the King's Guard that controlled the satellites, guns and various other munitions. The King's Guard were entrusted with the security of the Kingdom. Gabriel knew the importance of the King's Guard very well. He was the director.

Money had long ago been recognized as the root of all evil and dispensed with permanently. There was no currency, no derivatives and no financial markets. The right people had been appointed for the right jobs and performed them efficiently with integrity and purposefulness to ensure no one was taken advantage of and no one was deprived of their fair share of health and happiness.

Another reason for the state of well-being was the elimination of the bad ego, arrogance augmented by ignorance. Yet each individual felt they had self-worth, respect and a place in society. All that was expected in return for the bountiful provisions was loyalty to the Great King, who was the architect of the system and the provider, and to obey the laws he set forth. The Great King knew the degree of goodness in everyone and ranked them based on the jobs they performed in the Kingdom. Provisions were distributed in accordance with each person's rank, yet even the person with the lowest rank enjoyed plentiful share.

Life was so good. For a moment Gabriel wondered how long this would last. but then quickly dismissed the thought. Negativity would only get him in trouble. He knew that even a little bit of unhappiness could not survive in this happy environment. In fact it was the absence of negativity that had created this euphoric society of which he was proudly a part of. The King's Guard had the power to quickly and effectively deal with any rebellion, but the best way to ensure and maintain the current system was to keep the citizens genuinely happy. For that, happiness could not be dependent on temporary material luxuries and other hedonistic distractions but had to come from within. And that was exactly what was happening. With those thoughts in mind, Gabriel lay back and fell asleep.

It was then that his daydreaming was cut short and he was awakened by Jake. Then there was the surprise of the red smoke signal.

On the other side of the city, Assistant Director of the King's Guard, Michael Hartman, was suddenly shaken from his sleep by the sharp ringing of his private cell phone. This was an emergency number and only one person knew it.

"Gabriel," he said as he picked up the phone, "is everything okay?"

"Better hurry to the King's Council room. I just saw the red smoke signal," replied Gabriel.

Michael ran out to his living room, which faced the Great Palace and looked out of the window. He could not remember the last time he had seen red smoke. Quickly, he dressed and was headed out his apartment door, down the elevator and outside on his way to the royal court.

Both he and Gabriel had a pretty good handle on things, but this time they had no clue. Had they missed something? Perhaps it was some new directive meant for just him and Gabriel from the King. What was so important that it could not wait until the next morning?

CHAPTER TWO

THE KING'S PALACE SAT ON EIGHT HUNDRED square miles of rolling hills to the north of the Capital City. It lay in the northernmost part of the Kingdom and sat between the Sea of Aquatic Marvels to the east and the Forest of Wonders to the west. The palace boasted an expansive courtyard, the size of sixteen football fields made with olive green octagonal marble tiles inlaid with rubies and black sapphires. Each tile had edges made of gold. Ponds and water fountains adorned its octagonal perimeter. Winged angelic creatures flew around the courtyard singing praises of the King, their wings flapping ever so softly yet enough to gently activate the wind chimes, chimes that were suspended in mid-air without any support. Due to the large number of angelic creatures and the frequency and timeliness with which they flapped their wings, wind buoyancy was created for the wind chimes to keep afloat.

There was the sweet melody of a harp playing in every one of the octagonal courtyard's eight corners. In each corner, an angelic creature played a soothing tune in perfect harmony with the other harps. When the tune ended, the angelic creatures would look upwards as if looking for information on what tune to play next, and they would all begin playing the next segment suddenly. Every hour the tune would change, and they would rarely repeat a tune.

Visitors from the Forest of Wonders were a regular occurrence in the palace courtyard and grounds. Deer, flamingos and peacocks wandered the neatly manicured gardens and feasted on the lush vegetation around its edges. A fountain on the west side served as Jake's personal watering hole. He loved to roll around on his back and get wet, so he could then bask in the warm sun and dry off on a side bench nearby. The hoopoe would fly back and forth to deliver the King's messages to Ronaldo the Lion. Jake took his job very seriously but never passed the opportunity to enjoy himself whenever he could. One of his favourite pastimes was to fly a thousand miles across to the Sea of Aquatic Marvels, past the rows of mansions, over the sunkissed beaches and yacht filled marinas, to swoop down and piggyback on a blue whale. He would tickle the whale with his beak and found it particularly exciting when the whale took a dive. Jake would hold on until the last minute and then fly off into the deep blue sky barely escaping the whales' spout. It was adventurous, it was fun and it fitted Jake's lifestyle very well.

On the north side of the Palace there was the seven-tiered Garden Terrace adorned with white, red and yellow roses. Set against the backdrop of the northern lights, the Garden Terrace needed no illumination. As the northern lights darted around in a frenzied state across the sky, they projected a beautiful hue of blues, greens and pinks on the garden and bathed it in a mystical glow.

A kaleidoscope of colours covered the gardens and gave it a magical appearance. Each level of the Garden had different fruit trees and an aroma of jasmine, lavender, orange or cedar wood. Every now and then an angelic creature would swoop down and pickup a ripe pear or peach right off the tree. Somehow they always knew when it was the very moment to pick the fruit. There were water fountains on either side. Along the middle of the garden ran a stream the length of all seven gardens, and it was fed by a waterfall at the very top. Advanced engineering used gravity to supply the force as the water moved down through each of the seven levels, so no water pumps were necessary. This eliminated any interruption or maintenance and kept the water flowing. Bees were busy flying between the trees and flowers in the gentle westerly wind from the sea. The Rosewater River, named for its pink hue and scented water, ran around Garden Terrace, through the palace grounds to the south and fed into a large lagoon inhabited by resplendent swans. A drawbridge over the river led to the main entrance to the palace.

The most imposing part of the palace was the massive dome made of solid gold with a small glass window at the very top. About five miles in diameter, the dome was held up by nineteen granite pillars resting on a concrete slab containing the Eternity Meditation Chamber. Here the righteous servants of the King, having spent a lifetime of obedience and performance of duties, came to meditate towards the end of their earthly life below the dome. The Eternity Meditation Chamber was a great mystery to many because no one had been inside and come back out to describe its interior. Apparently, those who entered it received such an indescribable spiritual satisfaction that they decide to stay there until the very end. Five hundred and seventy feet above them, from the centre of the dome, shone a mystical bluish green light that stretched upwards in a straight line, through the window at the top to the sky, and extended into the heavens beyond as far as the eye could see. It was a kind of energy field unlike any other in the Kingdom. Frequently, angelic creatures would crowd around this little window and every now and then one of them attempted to climb the energy beam. They quit after a few minutes of trying because the energy was so intense, and they could not bear its presence.

Rumours abound about the Eternity Meditation Chamber and what lay inside. Some believed it contained a staircase to heaven. Others thought it was a very sombre place of meditation as the name suggested, amidst austere surroundings. Then there were others who speculated that it contained lavish treasures. Whatever lay inside, everybody wanted to retreat one day to it, but it was only accessible when the drawbridge came down, and that was reserved for a special vehicle at a specific time. Admittance was strictly restricted to occupants of a red, double-decker bus that arrived at 7 p.m. every night.

Even though everyone really wanted to go to the Eternity Meditation Chamber, they waited their turn. They knew that when the right time came, when they had developed themselves and deserved it, they would not be deprived of it. Instead, they tried ever so hard to be good citizens and perform their duties for the king.

* * * *

When he arrived at the drawbridge connecting the palace to the rest of the Great Kingdom, Gabriel realized that the bridge was raised.

"Quite unusual, they are expecting me. Must be that they are preoccupied with some important matter at hand."

Just then the clock struck seven p.m., and he heard the humming sound of a perfectly tuned engine. He turned around to see a bright red double-decker bus approaching. It seemed more like a party bus, bright red with young people cheering and taking photos. The drawbridge started coming down slowly. As Gabriel Bollinger sprinted across the drawbridge and up the stately set of stone stairs that led into the Golden Dome of the King's palace, he heard brisk footsteps behind him and realized that Michael Hartman was at his heels.

"It's been ages since we had a red smoke signal. Wonder what it could be?" Michael said from behind.

Deep in thought, Gabriel did not answer. He knew it was something serious. As far back as he could recollect, there was no mention of a red smoke signal ever having been issued.

Finally he replied tersely, "I know."

The pair made their way into the Chamber of the King's Council. Zachariah Papadopoulos sat at the head of an enormous rectangular mahogany table, his hands folded in front of him. His features were very distinct: a pointed nose, slightly hunched over and sporting a goatee. He had served the King well by delivering his messages. High above them, the black ceiling was dotted with what seemed like a million stars that gave out sparkling white light. At the centre of the table, above them hung a grandiose chandelier that lighted up the Chamber of the King's Council. The chandelier did not generate is own light but merely reflected the light of the stars above it through its crystals. The stone walls depicted beautiful pictures of the King's favourite birds and animals.

Zachariah was staring at an envelope in front of him. *Most unusual*, he thought as he remembered the instructions that accompanied the letter. *I wonder what is so secretive that the letter has to be sealed. I have never been given a sealed envelope before.*

He recalled how he had received the letter a little more than an hour ago. It was the same way he had received previous letters. There would be a knock on the door of his study, a door that led to the Meditation Chamber and was always locked from the other side. It had not been opened for centuries. The caretaker of the Meditation Chamber would pass him the letter through the mail slot. As far as Zachariah knew, the letters were picked up from the Emerald Basket, in the centre of the Meditation Chamber.

From the descriptions he had heard of the Emerald Basket, it had a greenish blue hue and was encased in a concave mirrored glass container that had a strange light at its centre. No one knew where the fuel for this light came from. The light radiated outward and magnified through the glass container to provide enough light for the entire seven hundred and fifty thousand square foot room. It was Zachariah's dream that one day when his work in the Kingdom was finished, he would go there and experience the aura of this light and the spiritual enlightenment it provided.

Gabriel and Michael slipped into the stuffed high-back red leather chairs on either side of Zack Papa, as they fondly called the old man. Seeing that he was involved in deep thought and had not even noticed their entrance, they chose not to disturb him. An uneasy silence began to unfold.

This is most unlike Papa, thought Michael Hartman. *He always greets us with a smile and gestures us to take a seat beside him. Must be something serious.* He turned to look at Gabriel sitting across with a stern look on his face and recalled his terse answer as they were crossing the drawbridge. *This must be very serious.*

He wished someone would break the silence soon. After what seemed like an eternity, actually it was hardly two minutes, Zack unfolded his arms, raised his head and reached for the envelope in front of him on the table.

He looked straight at Gabriel and said, "See this envelope? I received it about two hours ago. Even I do not know the contents of this envelope. But it came with instructions that it is to be given to you and not to be opened until the right time."

"What is the right time?" said Gabriel. Zack replied, "Honestly, I do not know."

"But how will I know when it is the right time?" Gabriel enquired, a little perplexity sounding in his voice.

As head of the King's Guard, he knew that it had to be a matter of national security. "That is what seems unusual to me, along with the fact that I don't know what is in the envelope," replied Zachariah. "The King would not have said this unless it would become pretty obvious. I assure you that you will know when it is the right time. Take this envelope and keep it in a safe place until you see a sign that the moment to open the envelope has arrived."

CHAPTER THREE

LUCIANO VARGAS PACED NERVOUSLY UP AND DOWN the covered verandah of his modest two-storey villa, the smoke from his cigar billowing up to the roof. He had some difficult decisions to make. He had worked hard for many years to climb the ladder and gain favour with the King. Yet he felt he could have done better and should have gained more recognition. Now he felt stuck in this job, and it seemed he was going nowhere. Somehow he felt he had been treated unfairly. Year after year his performance ratings were a dismal average.

Vargas, a podgy short man, was the mayor of Hellenbach. The town of Hellenbach lay deep in the Valley of the Palisades in zone 14666. Nestled in a remote area at the edge of a jungle, it did not attract much attention. There were no outstanding citizens or notable mentions to make it newsworthy. Many a traveller had passed by it without even noticing the town. It was the one part of the Kingdom that very few had ever heard of. Yet it lay there, a peaceful town with broad tree-lined avenues and white brick houses with red tiled roofs, just like any other small town in the southern part of the Kingdom.

The citizens of Hellenbach enjoyed all the privileges of the Kingdom. Provisions were delivered to the doorsteps of the inhabitants. Medical problems, far and few, were promptly taken care of by the Department of Well-Being. Citizens could travel freely and enjoy the beautiful parks and lakes.

As he walked back and forth along the verandah, a feeling of frustration and anger crept into Luciano Vargas's mind. He was not going to feel sorry for himself any more. Although he wanted more power, the King saw fit to keep him there. He was stagnating. Something had to be done. Surely he could manage a bigger zone. He was more determined than ever to get what he wanted. A hint of jealousy crept into Luciano. The King had it all, and he had so little. Why could he not get a little more? The only solution seemed to be independence from the Kingdom. Then he could do a better job of managing Hellenbach and earn the King's respect, a respect he thought he truly deserved. In order to secede he needed support from some key individuals and a plan that would work. Only then could he keep his subjects happy and perhaps not even be held accountable.

Luciano knew that he could never win a fight against the powerful King's Guard. He had to beat the King at his own game. The King cherished freedom for his subjects and all in the Kingdom were there only because they wanted to be there. Suddenly a novel idea dawned upon him.

The King has stated that freedom is the greatest gift he has given to his subjects. Let me challenge that, he thought. *Why don't I hold an election where the townsfolk vote whether or not they want to stay in the Kingdom and fix the results, so it is in my favour.*

The very thought of doing this unrighteous deed made him feel guilty. After a lot of soul searching Luciano finally did something no one had ever done before in the Kingdom. He succumbed to the idea of not just holding an election, but rigging it as well. He chose evil over good.

"The end justifies the means, I know the people will be happier," he said aloud as he finally walked indoors and reached for the telephone. "I will win even if I have to manipulate the results of the election."

Luciano knew he could not openly rig the elections, but he could play a propaganda war, spread misinformation and use his power of persuasion by convincing the people that life under his rule would actually be better for them. After all, the King was ruling from a distance and Luciano with his hands-on approach was more in touch with the people's needs and could meet their needs faster and better. Luciano argued, "since no one has seen the King, I could convince people that he is not there anymore. Perhaps he does not even exist, except in people's minds, and this entire system has evolved by itself randomly through pure chance."

* * * *

Steven Schneider and Alistair Johnson had gotten a call from Luciano Vargas the night before. The mayor had sounded very excited when he told them he had something important to discuss which would greatly benefit them. They had a close working relationship with the Mayor and also a friendship built over many years. Luciano, they felt, was someone who could be trusted. Being his lieutenants, they had some clout in getting things done on behalf of the mayor, and he had always appreciated their help.

Steven turned his white BMW onto Central Street and slid the vehicle close to the curb in front of the mayor's white villa. As the vehicle came to a halt, he turned towards Alistair with a sense of optimism.

"Luciano sounded so excited. He must have figured out a way to better our lives."

Alistair sounded doubtful. "I don't know, maybe we should be happy with what we have. The King gives us everything we need, and I am afraid we may be getting greedy."

Shaking his head Steven said, "Alistair, there is nothing wrong with bettering ourselves and wanting more. Let us at least hear him out."

They walked around the side of the house and slipped through the fence door. As they made their way across the backyard lawn, they saw Luciano was seated in the gazebo. A table lay in front of him laden with truffle covered marzipan pastries, a variety of brie cheese, chicken kabobs on skewers and shrimp dumplings The aroma of freshly brewed coffee filled the air. When they entered, Luciano got up to greet them warmly and asked them to be seated across the table on the deeply cushioned deck chairs.

After a few pleasantries, Luciano sensing their nervousness offered them refreshments. Then he got straight to the point. He knew he had to sell them on an idea even if it was grossly exaggerated. He could pull it off, and then they would see it was not a lie. He knew they had the right contacts and had to convince them to hold a referendum. He knew some of the people were isolated and ignorant, and he could sell them on his idea. The rest would follow based on peer pressure. Even though he again felt guilty, he quickly shrugged away the feeling and convinced himself that the end justified the means.

Luciano had selected Steven and Alistair because he knew their weaknesses as well as their strengths. They were good obedient soldiers who needed leadership, guidance and a sense of purpose. He had at times sensed an expression of dissatisfaction from them, even a hint of objection. These traits were so uncommon among the people that Luciano, a shrewd observer of behaviour, noticed them at once. Surely, he could sow these seeds of discontent and use them to his advantage.

"Listen guys, you know my record, and you know I would only do what is good for our zone. Don't you think we are mature capable adults who can make the right decisions about what it is we want and what is good for us?" Steven and Alistair waited a moment and then both nodded. Luciano continued, "We get only measured provisions, and while we have a great deal of freedom, we cannot do whatever we want. I for one would like to have a bigger house, a pool in the backyard, perhaps even a chef and butler. Wouldn't you?"

There was a moment of silence then Alistair responded with some trepidation. "Are you not being greedy? After all we are all quite happy where we are."

"My dear Alistair," said Luciano, his voice brimming with genuine caring, "there is nothing wrong with wanting more as long as it is not hurting anyone. Let us not stick to ideals, let us be practical. We have never really been motivated because we get everything we need. We could enhance our lives in many ways. Don't underestimate the power of motivation and hard work. We have been pampered and spoilt, and it shows in our underachievement."

Luciano gave Steven and Alistair a minute to absorb what he had said. Sensing that it had them thinking, and that no further resistance was being offered, he said, "And let's not just think about ourselves.

It is not about us, it is about the people. I feel we would be letting them down and I could not live with my conscience if I failed them."

Steven spoke up. "Luciano, this sounds risky. The King has enormous power. We cannot have him being angry with us. What if--"

Before Steven could finish Luciano quickly cut him off. "Let's be positive. The King has always been a kind King and we are showing no disrespect to him. He wants us to be happy and has given us what he cherishes for his subjects: the gift of free will and free choice. If we decide we want to make it on our own, he will not interfere. Maybe we can show him what a great job we can do, and perhaps he may allow other zones to make it on their own or even join us. This may be the beginning of something wonderful."

"Okay so what do you want us to do?" Steven and Alistair said almost simultaneously.

"Well, we simply do the groundwork and hold a referendum. Let us not make a big show in case word gets out and the King finds out. Mostly door to door canvassing and then a day when people cast their votes."

Alistair and Steven seemed convinced, even a little excited, that the mayor had come up with a no risk progressive option. He had seemed very forthright and reasonable and the idea was actually quite good.

"Sounds easy, we will start working on this right away," said Stephen, and the two of them got up, shook Luciano's hand, thanked him for his hospitality and left.

Steven and Alistair went to work almost immediately. They rented a printing press and designed and printed ballots. They passed out leaflets about an upcoming referendum that would allow the citizens more room to negotiate provisions. Door to door canvassing was done at quiet times of the afternoon, so as not to attract much attention. Voting booths were set up in private places with small signs that were hardly noticeable. Lists of deceased persons and visitors who had stayed temporarily were acquired and added to the electorate database so that the referendum results would be titled in the favour of yes, no matter how the actual voting went.

* * * *

It was 3 a.m. and Luciano Vargas tossed and turned in bed. He was sweating and very anxious. Four months had passed since he had the backyard meeting with Steven and Alistair. They had done a tremendous job of organizing and holding a referendum. The polls had closed last night and the results were forthcoming within the hour.

Luciano jumped out of bed when he heard the phone ring. It was Steven Schneider. He sounded very excited.

"We got the referendum passed by an overwhelming majority." They had worked very hard and had won over the people. "As we speak, there is an announcement being made on local TV about the results."

"Congratulations to you, my new Chief of Staff," Luciano said boldly. "Great job you and Alistair have done."

"And to you too, Mr. President," replied Steven with a slight tone of hesitancy in his voice.

Luciano sprang to life. Now he had to make a public statement to declare independence of zone 14666 and inform the King. This was the day Luciano had been dreaming of for a very long time, but he knew it would not be an easy task. He would have to work very hard to satisfy his people and prove to the King that he had taken a wise step. If he failed, there would be dire consequences, but he was not going to fail. Of that, he was sure.

The first order of the day was to call his lieutenants and plan a meeting to form a committee that would put together a council of ministers. They would then make a Constitution and formulate a five-year plan on how the new nation was going to operate, to move forward with and fund projects essential to stability and prosperity. There was so much to be done in nation building.

CHAPTER FOUR

IT WAS EARLY SATURDAY MORNING. GABRIEL prepared a concoction of his favourite pomegranate juice with a hint of honey and topped it off with rose water. He stretched himself out on the deck chair and looked towards the mysterious green energy beam that rose upward from the centre of the Meditation Room in the King's palace. He wondered where it led to. Having never seen the King, or knowing where the King was, he had resigned himself to the fact that there were certain mysteries he would just have to contend with.

Suddenly he heard Jake's voice, "Hello Monsignor." Jake had a habit of changing languages and putting on different accents. Usually he would use a southern drawl because he knew that made Gabriel chuckle, but this time he sounded different. He sounded Irish.

"What's up Jake? Is it not kind of early?" said Gabriel, sitting up to face the hoopoe. "What brings you here?"

"Oh nothing really," replied the bird, "Just came over to say hi." Gabriel felt something was not quite right. "And to tell you something exciting happened yesterday," continued Jake.

Gabriel knew there was something going on so he prodded Jake. "Tell me what happened. I hope Ronaldo did not have one of his tantrums and try to make lunch meat out of you."

Jake laughed. "No nothing like that. Gabriel, you do have a wild imagination. Are you hungry?"

Gabriel knew that Jake was a politician, adept at evading questions and deflecting criticism. The hoopoe had quite a personality, a colourful character - boisterous sometimes, coy at other times. He could never win an argument with Jake, but he also knew Jake was genuine and behind the act that he put on was a compassionate, caring bird with a high sense of integrity.

"Then what?" Gabriel persisted.

"I was riding on the back of Bella, the humpback whale when she decided to go for a dive. Naturally I took off, but this time I was a bit slow and the spout almost drowned me. I felt my life was being dragged from my throat, but luckily I landed back on Bella, took a minute to gather my strength and then flew off."

Gabriel grinned. "My feathery friend, if you don't get out of the fast lane, you are going to die young, and I am going to miss you. Now scoot off and take it easy."

As the bird took off towards the warm southern sky, Gabriel reclined back, sipped his drink and let his thoughts of Jake's most recent adventure entertain him.

It was about an hour later when Gabriel woke up and started to return indoors. A piece of paper caught his eye. It was one of the messages that Jake carried, tied to his leg but it had somehow become unattached. With a twist of fate, the paper had unrolled itself. A picture of a neatly drawn timepiece was on the slip. Gabriel could not believe his eyes.

"Omigosh," he exclaimed. He had almost forgotten about the envelope. "It is time to open the King's letter!"

He rushed inside to where the envelope was safely tucked, under the mat on his bedside stand. A rush of strange feelings overcame him - nervousness, hesitation, excitement and anxiety mixed with fear. Did he read the signal correctly? Jake had been acting strange, what with this story of almost drowning. Jake had ridden on the backs of whales for years and was no amateur. Of all the whales that Gabriel had heard of, Bella was the most mature, stable and predictable. She would never do anything to endanger the life of Jake. Besides, Jake never visited him on Saturdays. He had too many other extra-curricular activities.

This was not a matter for the weak at heart. He was the director of the King's Guard. He had to make a decision, the right decision. Was he opening the letter prematurely? Had he read the sign correctly?

Gabriel opened the letter. It was a royal decree with the official stamp of the King. He began to read it. Six hundred metres above him, with the breeze gently blowing across his wings, Jake circled and peered through Gabriel's bedroom window.

"I knew he would figure it out," he muttered and then, after making a 270 degree turn, went on his way sailing skyward through the wind.

> My subjects, I am your King. There is no other King. Your every need is provided for. You have security, abundant provisions and happiness. There is no greed, no jealousy and no vice. Lives and property are respected. Freedom is my most cherished gift to you - freedom of travel, speech, economy and belief.

> I am just, fair and benevolent. All I expect from my subjects is loyalty and appreciation.
>
> I have known for a long time that the mayor of zone 14666, Luciano Vargas, has had supercilious thoughts that he can be a king and manage his own dominion. There is much more to being a king than he can imagine. When you open this letter, Gabriel, he and his supporters will have just declared independence. I have a plan to counter his schemes.

Gabriel lifted his head and stared out the window. He wondered, *If the King knew this was going to happen why did he not stop Luciano until now.* Then he started reading again.

> You might wonder why I allowed Luciano to go this far since I knew what he was going to do for a very long time. You, Gabriel may wonder why I never asked you to overpower and bring him in. It is because he will complain that he was denied his freedom, and all the other people will wonder why I did this. Even those in other parts of the Kingdom will wonder. Yet others will believe that he can be a king and may want to see a test of his ability.
>
> Yet I cannot let things stand as they are because Luciano is trying to trick people with false promises, and has claimed a share of them. If allowed to continue unabated, he will deceive them even more. There is no point trying to convince him that he cannot be a king.

He is stubborn, unwise and arrogant, and that will be his downfall. The best way to solve this argument is to let him try to be a king and fail.

The simplest thing to do is imprison or banish the rebels from the Kingdom, thought Gabriel.

The letter continued: We can just overpower all of them, punish or banish them, and we can very easily bring our formidable forces to do that. The most efficient solution is to give Luciano a tiny kingdom, and when he cannot even manage this without misery, chaos, disease and wars, he will prove his own incompetence to anyone who harbours the idea of running their own show.

To be a king, Luciano needs subjects. They are the ones who think he can be a king. It all comes back to freedom and wanting to be in my Kingdom. I do not want to force those people to be here if they do not want to. So you see, Gabriel, this is not just about Luciano, it is much bigger. Since they and you have only known good and take it for granted, my plan is to create the definition of evil and then point out the right and wrong paths to them, but for this, they have to be outside the Kingdom, on their own and free to choose. Evil cannot exist in my Kingdom and neither can unhappiness. For in my Kingdom there is only good. Those who choose good are with me. Those who choose evil are with Luciano. I want to give them another chance to realize their error. There are some good souls who were swayed by peer pressure and do not deserve banishment forever. The ones that fail the test will forever be banished from my Kingdom. The punishment must fit the crime. Only the most ardent opponents will be punished and deprived of the joys of being in my Kingdom. As for those who decide to hold fast to my laws and realize only I can be king, they will be redeemed back into my Kingdom.

Gabriel started wondering what his role in all this was.

So this is my plan, a plan I want you to execute, Gabriel. Go to them with your forces and bring all those who side with Luciano and oppose you. Many will realize their mistake and repent for their mistakes. Some of them will try and resist but will fail. Don't put them in prison because that will serve no purpose. We don't need overcrowded prisons that are a burden on the system. Take all of them, except Luciano, to the Department of Well-Being. There is a special area that has been designated for them, and staff has been instructed to be waiting for them. The staff will put them to sleep and use AAC to modify the gene controlling their minds, so as to remove all memories of the rebellion from their thoughts.

They will then be transported to the middle of the Barren Lands at the southern fringes of the Kingdom, where they will be awakened. We will give them the know-how and the resources to build their kingdom, a tiny kingdom by my standards, with Luciano as a ruler. Even though they are rebels, and deserve prison, I am gracious and merciful and will allow them a beautiful place where they can grow fruits and vegetables, have houses with furnishings and gardens, and livestock, crops and meat of birds for food. We will allow the bees to pollinate the trees so they can have beautiful flowers and delicious fruits of all kinds. They can create entertainment for themselves and modes of transportation for convenience. For a hundred million miles in either direction, they will see nothing outside their kingdom. As far as they are concerned, there is no other life elsewhere. As for those who realize their mistake and repent, they will serve the rebels in various capacities and then get redeemed back into my Kingdom after serving their purpose.

What about Luciano, Gabriel thought.

As for Luciano, I have reached an agreement with him. He will be respited for 6000 years, and given the chance to run the tiniest of kingdoms, after which he will be banished forever from my Kingdom. During that time, he is allowed to mislead those who are egoistic and have a tendency to be greedy. They are the ones who will be preoccupied with lesser matters, rather than the purpose of their existence in the tiny kingdom. The only condition is that he keep the knowledge of the rebellion to himself. For his own sake he will keep it private otherwise his subjects will condemn him for taking them out of my Kingdom and into the middle of nowhere instead of the happy life they led here.

I have already set up a tiny kingdom for him, a circle with a twenty-five thousand mile radius, complete with essential ecosystems to provide food, water, shelter and clothing for his people. They will start off by cutting the trees for building materials and fire for cooking and then progress to building super highways with cement and buildings of steel. We will watch them with our invisible, stealth based AAC satellites and see every move they make and every scheme they devise. To help the deserving, I will send emissaries with knowledge and wisdom. Some will accept but a majority of them will side with Luciano's law and commit evil."

Gabriel was flabbergasted. This letter was mind-boggling. It seemed that every thought he had, every question he raised in his mind was answered immediately in the letter. The King knew every plan and every move he was going to make beforehand! As unnerving as it sounded, he quickly calmed himself and called Michael to explain what the King's Guard was about to do next.

CHAPTER FIVE

THE PRESIDENT'S SUMMER RETREAT WAS SITUATED on the banks of the Snake River. Situated in a scenic valley nestled between snow-clad mountains, the river twisted and wound around like a snake until it reached the mouth of Lake Vargas. Boasting a twelve thousand square feet marble-tiled octagonal courtyard, the gold-plated, domed palace was surrounded by lush gardens adorned with statues of Luciano and ponds embellished with swans. The side of the palace facing the river was like a wall of glass, offering the occupants sweeping views of the river and the mountains. Sweet relaxing music played through hidden speakers throughout the courtyard. Luciano had tried to mimic the great palace of the king as best he could. On the other side of the river lay hundreds of acres of vineyards owned by the president.

The Governing Council of Luceville met at the president's summer retreat in the lavishly decorated private chambers of President For Life, Luciano Vargas. At the head of the large stone table sat Luciano Vargas, dressed in full military uniform, his attire proudly displaying his medal of valour. On the wall behind him hung several photographs of his distinguished military career and victories in battle. On his right were the Minister of Finance and the Chief of Staff of the Armed Forces. On his left sat the Minister of Health and the Minister of Sports & Entertainment. Also present were the Ministers of Agriculture and Construction.

Luciano had hand-picked people to his Governing Council and had entrusted them with the responsibility of developing plans for their respective ministries. He had to form and run a kingdom where his subjects were happy yet where he could gather enormous wealth for himself. The whole idea was to create an illusion, and keep people so distracted that they would not question the system. While he knew what he really wanted from the system, he was careful to put it across to his ministers as something that would be for the general good of all his subjects. "Keep the people busy through distractions, and make them feel good and they will submit to whatever I propose for them," he figured.

"Gentlemen," Luciano began, "this is a historic occasion where we are deciding on the course of our republic. We have to set our goals and policies so we can implement projects that will make our country a shining example of what wise leadership, hard work and efficient planning can accomplish. Even though I am your president, this is a democratic institution, and I will listen to each and every one of you and give serious consideration to your suggestions. Please present me with your plans for our new nation."

One by one the ministers read off their policy statements and the plans associated with them.

The amalgamated plan would first create a paper currency, as advised by the president, to facilitate economic transactions. There would be a Central Bank that would print and control the money supply and lend money to banks. Through financing from the banks, massive construction projects would start. Roadways and flyovers, office towers, shopping malls and housing developments would be built. Manufacturing would be started to produce everything from raw materials to finished goods. Airplanes, ships and tanks would be produced. There would be a stock exchange set up for trading stocks and commodities.

Originally the plan had called for the introduction of currency backed by precious metals like gold or silver, but Luciano had opposed that idea. He had vast holdings of precious metals and did not want to risk jeopardizing these in case depositors made a rush to exchange their currency to precious metals. Besides, the banks could print a lot more money if it were not backed by precious metals. More money meant more interest income. He had sold this idea to the finance minister by convincing him that economic development would proceed faster and on a larger scale if the bank had the freedom to print money without a resource-backed currency.

To protect people's lives and properties, there would be an insurance industry. Medical health benefits would be available for those who had medical insurance. People would get education at institutions of learning and find jobs where they could pursue careers in different fields in the industries that would be set up. Then there would be the military industrial complex, the news media and the entertainment industry consisting of television, sports and gambling.

At the political level, the republic would be divided into 15 autonomous regions, each with its own elected government and military. Each region would have its own sports teams in basketball, baseball, football and hockey.

Projects and social programs would be paid by taxing the income of businesses and individuals. Unemployment and old age pension benefits would be financed by their respective premium collections while sports initiatives would be supported by lottery and gambling.

Property taxes would pay for schools. Higher education would require taking a loan from the government with lower rates and easier payment options.

After the presentation of the amalgamated plan, Luciano looked at Chief of staff, Steven Schneider, who gave an approving nod.

He then stood up and smiled. "I thank you gentlemen for a job well done. I am very satisfied with this plan and by presidential decree, approve it into existence. Let us move ahead immediately with the implementation of these historic institutions that are critical to our national interest."

Luciano adjourned the meeting and dismissed the General Council. He walked back into the lavish king's quarters, slipped into some comfortable clothing and relaxed on a chaise in front of a huge marble fireplace. He beckoned to his butler and soon the butler arrived with a tray of smoked salmon and prime rib medallions surrounded by multi grain crackers and freshly baked pumpernickel bread, and aged white wine. Soon another tray arrived consisting of Thyme-Braised Duck Legs with Chanterelle mushrooms and potatoes, and marsala chicken with amaretto sauce. As Luciano feasted on this sumptuous meal, he was quickly joined by two scantily clad girls clad in bathing suits, who had just emerged from the indoor swimming pool across the hallway.

This was going to be great, thought Luciano. *No one to hold me accountable, a fresh start. I can build and create. I can also destroy what interferes with my plans.*

He smiled to himself at having pulled off one of the biggest scams by passing the amalgamated rejuvenation plan. This was a master stroke of genius. He was the con man extraordinaire.

What the Governing Council and the people would never know is how the plan would benefit Luciano and make him wealthy beyond imagination. Every aspect of the plan offered the opportunity to generate money for him, but he had to be smart. "But then I have always been smart and outwitted those around me," he thought.

Luciano had based his plan on fear and insecurity while creating an illusion of well-being and health. This was capitalism at its meanest while appearing to be a socialist state providing benefits to the average person. With a few select individuals cashing in, he would get part of the pie - a pie that he would have all his fingers in. He could not get his mind off the enormous revenue stream that was about to flow in. Printing money would create instant wealth and then lending this money out on interest would create more wealth.

Interest income on every house, yacht, car, business and student loan. Sales tax on every purchase made. Income tax on every penny earned, he dreamed *One day I might even be wealthier than the King, especially if I can carry this over to other zones.*

Luciano saw lots of other opportunities to make money. *If I sell treasury notes through the Central bank and use the money to take a controlling interest in the bricks and mortar companies, and insurance and media, I will make a killing.*

He knew as long as current demands for pension and unemployment benefits were met, and the roads were kept in decent shape and people could keep busy and distracted with TV and sports he could ride the wave. And by slowly reducing population lifespan through junk food and lack of exercise, the pension fund would have a healthy surplus especially if wisely invested through the banking system.

He loved the idea of paper currency. Initially, he may have to back it up with a commodity like gold. But eventually he could back it up against the future cash flows of taxes to be collected from the hard work of the people. Mortgage debt and other financial instruments could be bundled and sold off to investors to create a giant bubble that would grow in wealth. Reverse mortgages could be offered to those who built equity in their properties. People would work most of their lives to pay off their house mortgages and build equity, and he could then buy back that equity by offering them paper money. By varying interest rates, cycles of high and low values could be created which would create the perfect opportunity for banks and select investors to buy low, sell high and reap enormous profits.

Yet his most prized cash cow was to be the military industrial complex. By creating an atmosphere of fear and keeping tensions alive, he could sell arms to all those regions desperate to protect themselves for a very handsome profit. *Fifteen regions, each with its own navy, army and air force*, Luciano told himself almost snootily. While wars would be against his primary goal of being able to run a kingdom without chaos and misery, as a last resort, and to prevent stock piling and obsolescence of weapons, war would have to be an option and an ongoing process, if necessary. This could be done by creating a number of false flag operations and putting the blame on the wrong party and use that as an excuse to start a war. He would make them fight amongst themselves if he needed to. Wars always created a distraction from the real problems.

The media would play a pivotal role in spreading misinformation. While they would operate under the premise of freedom of speech, there would be censorship behind the scenes. Media executives would get rewarded with perks if they played along and punished with lack of access to newsworthy stories if they did not. Since they relied on advertising to stay in business and make profits, they could not afford to be denied privileged 'first-access' to breaking stories and rumours.

I could get the different regions to import and export goods and charge duty.

Luciano knew that federal grants and loans would have to be allocated in such a way that different regions would produce goods needed by one another in order to create demand, and opportunity for black marketing.

The climate of insecurity would cause a surge in demand for guns and security systems. *I could sell a gun to every household!* To top it all, Luciano had decided to produce beer and wine by fermenting the grapes from his vineyards. *It is great business and besides, nothing like a little bubbly to keep the folks happy.* He remembered his days back in the Great Kingdom as mayor of Hellenback, where he had fermented grapes and created some home-made wine for personal use. It had helped him forget about his worries.

At the end of the six thousand year period, if things were on the verge of collapsing, so what? His reign would be over, and he would have proved that he successfully managed a kingdom. Even if it backfired, it was so far in the future, and he would have a life of opulence until then, a life that he loved so much. Six thousand years of hedonistic living in a utopian environment and probably the King would still take him back. Luciano admired his position. *I have done well so far.* He just needed to carry out the plan to fruition. As long as he kept his subjects happy, and managed a kingdom without problems, he would have proved his competence to the King. If all else failed he could always beg the king for mercy and say he made a big mistake and should never have doubted the fact that only the king could actually run a dominion. Luciano felt satisfied that he had covered all the loose ends.

CHAPTER SIX

OVER FIFTY SEVEN HUNDRED YEARS HAD GONE BY and luciano was mentally reviewing how things had gone. It did not look good at all. Yes, he had done tremendously well for himself and had built a magnificent palace with a gold dome overlooking the lake, but he had not been able to keep his domain free of misery and chaos nor his subjects happy. A worried look hung over his face, but he had to try harder. He could not afford to fail. He was starting to have serious doubts about whether his scheme would work. What if he failed and the king did not take him back into his kingdom? He would be left with nothing. There was no alternative. He simply had to try harder, maybe with even more cunning than before. Luck had not been on his side, but he knew that he could do it. He could not afford to fail. Failure was not an option. His ego would not allow him to believe he was losing the battle.

Just in the last hundred years there had been plagues, several major earthquakes, tornadoes and floods. Heart disease and cancer were on the rise. New diseases were cropping up like type II diabetes. Crime and poverty were on the rise. Murders, burglaries and rape were becoming rampant. There had been a great depression that had left many penniless, and another one seemed likely in the next few years. Luciano mulled over his strategy and where he had gone wrong. A big culprit to the rise in crime were the alcoholic beverages that his factories were producing and selling.

Even the confidence in the stock market was fading due to insider trading and derivatives fraud. People were getting wary of the fiat currency, which was backed by citizens' ability to pay tax. Real estate cycles, based on interest rates were causing more foreclosures than ever before. There was even a grass-roots movement to get rid of the central bank but luckily the media kept that under tabs. Politicians were being looked upon as crooks. Public works were in severe jeopardy as greedy officials took bribes to give contracts to friends, who in turn did shoddy jobs to bolster profits. Even airlines were cutting back on maintenance as rising fuel costs and competition drove their profits down. Just in the last two months there had been three plane crashes attributed to possible maintenance oversights.

Luciano realized a big part of the problem. The people were becoming greedy. They wanted more and more. The artificial materialism of life he was providing was not enough. It actually became an addiction. The lust for power and control was increasing. When people could not get what they wanted, or what others had, they got desperate and resorted to crime or committed suicide. There was a voracious appetite for getting more by working less. It struck him that his subjects were becoming like him. He had to create more distractions and keep the illusion of wealth and happiness alive until he figured out how to rework his plan and make it successful. He had one big advantage. He had thousands of years of experience and always worked through his council. By staying in the shadows, he never took blame if things went wrong, but enjoyed the benefits and praises if his schemes succeeded.

What really worried Luciano was that even though the blame could not be assigned to him, his people would rebel against the system, the very one that was making him huge sums of money. Also a happy nation furthered his argument that he could handle a dominion by himself. Something had to be done urgently. Time was of the essence.

By creating artificial problems and then coming out with solutions he could manipulate the situation so that his policies would look good and his agents would look like saviours and heroes instead of the leeches they really were. Several new initiatives came into Luciano's mind and he started jotting down the ideas.

Drugs would be introduced into the inner cities. At the same time an official policy of a war on drugs would be maintained to keep the price high and provide black market opportunities. Intelligence services agents would sell the drugs, but others would be arrested for doing so. The poor and down trodden would be provided these, so they would live a life of illusion and stop complaining about not finding jobs - as long as they had the bare minimum to be able to buy the drugs. More police would be employed to control the drug problem and arrest violators. This would create additional employment opportunities in the judicial departments and prisons. There would be more and more media reports on how well the war on drugs was progressing.

New viruses would be developed in secret laboratories and unleashed on an unsuspecting public. As more people fell sick and died, a miracle cure in the form of a vaccine would be announced, touting the research and development grants by the government in combating these new threats to public health. Along with this there would be renewed appeals to the public to pledge more money towards ongoing research and development even as more drugs would be introduced into circulation. Luciano knew that the medical field and insurance complemented each other. The idea was not to prevent or cure illness, but just treat the symptoms by putting patients on a cyclical schedule of prescription drugs. By keeping the costs of these drugs high, a patient would be compelled to buy health insurance. The pharmaceutical companies and insurance companies would pay substantial taxes on their huge profits. To get healthy people sick was the issue he had to tackle next.

The food and water supply had to be contaminated. It was easy to infuse tap water with chlorine under the pretext that it would kill harmful bacteria present in water. The unpleasant taste of chlorine would lead people to other sources of water, giving birth to the bottled water industry. These bottles, made of plastic would cause more health problems. Natural foods would slowly have to be abandoned in favour of foods that were more convenient or promised better vitality, and could be produced with the economies of large scale production. A whole new set of foods would be created, filled with chemicals that the body would not recognize and not be able to process. But shelf life and profits would be greater. Eventually the organs would be overburdened with excess work and fail. As more people fell sick, doctors would work harder to save them. The plan was to keep people alive but sick, so they could go through the medical system, buy drugs and health insurance.

Another area Luciano had to look at was investments. He worried that one day the paper currency might lose its value. Inflation was already eroding what the money could buy. He was already the largest holder of gold and other precious metals and commodities, but he had to buy into the stocks of the major companies. Besides aircraft and car manufacturing, tech and financial stocks he had to get into more consumer goods, energy and telecom. By having his own people elected to the board of directors, he could exert greater influence in the running of these companies.

A worrisome thought occurred to Luciano. What if some of the fifteen regions decided to form a unified trading block? This would eliminate smuggling and tariffs in the economic union. It would also create a climate of peace, and that would be bad for the arms business. They may even secede. His creative mind soon devised a solution. He would have to hold a referendum and rig it so the union broke apart and then rain down financial misery on the dissidents. The people would blame themselves for their wrong decision and would decide to go back to the original system he had set in place. Once again, he would come out looking like a saviour. "I will divide and conquer."

Luciano seemed satisfied that he could achieve the above goals, but a new threat had emerged that he had not bargained for. It had to deal with the spiritual needs of his people, something he could not satisfy. He had allowed a thousand different churches to prosper and preach their individual brand of spirituality. This had worked quite well. Under the guise of freedom of religion, and the right of each person to make their own choice, he had managed to thoroughly confuse the nature of their existence in his kingdom. He had to counter the regular influx of emissaries sent by the Great King, emissaries that tried to raise awareness and appeal to the intellect of the people. The emissaries would come with some kind of sign, and tell the people to pledge allegiance to a great king that lived in a land far, far away, and brought a set of laws based on righteous principles that people could follow to live a perfect life. These emissaries were often totally rejected. Those that did believe them were persecuted or ridiculed by the rest and went into hiding, or were killed.

But this time it was different. Luciano had heard that the latest emissary came with not only a powerful sign but also answers to many questions that the people wanted to know, such as why they were there, where they were going and what they needed to do. Answers to questions that they never even dared to ask before because the answer seemed so distant. This emissary had come with mathematical proof, a code that could be demonstrated to be from outside his kingdom. Luciano knew that mixing truth with falsehood was a stronger weapon than just falsehood and this had worked quite well for him until now. He did not know how to counter this new threat.

He was the only one who knew about the rebellion in the Great Kingdom that resulted in him being given his own kingdom with subjects. He was the only one that had lived for the last six thousand years because his longevity gene had not been turned off. More than anything else, he had kept behind the scenes at all times so as to be practically invisible to all except the few that were in his council and his agents. He had used this to his fullest advantage, but now it seemed that the cat was out of the bag at last. This emissary knew about the covenant Luciano had made with the Great King. Unless he could stop it, things would really get out of control.

Desperate times called for desperate measures. This emissary would have to be eliminated. There was no other choice, no other way.

* * * *

Malcolm Johansen was on a special mission. As the Great King's emissary to the nation of Luceville, he had a challenge on his hands. He also had seven pear shaped beads arranged in perfect mathematical symmetry in his pocket as a sign of his authenticity, to help him on his assignment. His task was to preach to and convince those citizens of Luceville that would heed the information he was bringing about achieving perfect happiness, health, wealth and peace of mind and to make a successful transition back to the Great Kingdom.

Initially there was great joy when he presented the perfect symmetrical structure and beauty of the seven pears, and many people listened. The construction of the beads and what they implied gave a very powerful impression of what they represented. The clarity of his message was equally compelling. But gradually he became perceived as a threat by the establishment, those in power and in control of the churches, the financial structure and the military industrial complex. Complaints turned to ridicule and mocking and eventually to threats.

Malcolm was driving up to his sanctuary in the Rosalind Mountains, north of the capital, a place he frequented to meditate, when he was ambushed by Luciano's henchmen. They riddled his car with bullets and dragged him out and left him on the road to die. Then they took off on their motorcycles.

As he lay in the middle of the road, bleeding profusely and gasping for every breath, a feeling of submission came over him. He felt he could not hold on any longer, he simply had to let go. Just before he closed his eyes for the last time, he saw a bluish green beam that seemed to stretch down from the sky and connect to his forehead. Suddenly he could hear harps playing in the background and the words, "Welcome into My servants, welcome into My paradise." He felt he was being transported at a lightning fast speed up the beam. It was like the most beautiful dream he could imagine.

CHAPTER SEVEN

SEBASTIAN GIRARD NEVER NEEDED AN ALARM TO wake up in the morning. At precisely 7 a.m. every day, he could hear the whistling of the kettle as Gracie started to prepare breakfast in the kitchen of the two bedroom condo that they shared in downtown Los Angeles. Today seemed to start off as just another day, but it was no ordinary day. Sebastian had an important job interview.

Aunt Grace, affectionately called Gracie by Sebastian, was his mother's older sister. She had taken care of Sebastian ever since he was ten years old, after his parents, Adrian and Becky, had died in a horrific head-on collision in the mountains outside Denver while they were returning back from a ski vacation. They had both died at the young age of 38, and Aunt Grace had taken the young boy under her wing. Now Sebastian was twenty-four years old with a college degree. Aunt Grace, herself a sixty-nine year old widow without children dreaded the day when he would leave home, but she knew that day would come. Every passing day brought the inevitable closer. She had brought him up well and was confident he would always be around to help her.

Her brother-in-law, Adrian, had been a science professor at Berkeley and her sister, Becky, a physician's assistant at St. Vincent Medical Center. They both had loved nature and made frequent camping trips with their young son to Mount Pinos located in the Los Padres National Forest about an hour away. At 8831 feet, Mount Pinos was a popular destination for star gazers. It also offered camping and hiking trails. As they would sit around a campfire, huddled in blankets on a cold fall night, Adrian would point out certain stars and tell the younger Girard their names and approximate distances. Adrian would bring along his 10" telescope, so his curious son could see the bright colours in the Andromeda Galaxy and the Orion Nebula. They would focus on the planets and count them. The huge distances and twinkling lights never ceased to amaze the youngster. He admired how the stars got up there and why they appeared every night in the same place. Were they trying to tell him something? Mysteries of the universe intrigued him. Whenever Becky got time from her work and relieved from house chores she sat and read to him about the wonderful design of the human body, the organs, the senses and the emotions associated with it. This further fascinated Sebastian. The fact that there were about seventy trillion cells in the body, each performing functions from birth to death and the inner workings of the RNA, mitochondria, protein synthesis and transfer of genetic information were mind-boggling. Adrian explained how the sun generated light. There were millions of nuclear explosions taking place in the sun that released energy. The energy generated at the centre of the sun took forty years to reach its surface and only eight minutes to reach the Earth. On its way here, a lot of the harmful energy was blocked and only 3 percent of the light, called visible light actually reached the human eye. It was this light that brought to life the millions of shades of different colours that we were able to observe around us. Sebastian found this most fascinating.

Then there was the moon and its unique design. It did not generate its own light but simply reflected the light of the sun. Due to the unique and accurate positioning of the earth, sun and moon, the visible portion of the moon that was not covered in shadow served as a timing device. For centuries people had been able to tell the month and day of the year by simply looking at it. He questioned if there was a Creator who was behind all this and whether there was a purpose behind the creation.

After the loss of his parents, Sebastian often wondered if they had gone to a better place, and if he would ever meet them again. It did not seem impossible. Many of his friends in college did not believe in resurrection, but he reasoned that if he was created once, he could be resurrected again. After all, the initial creation was a form of resurrection - nothingness or death followed by life. Having been brought up in the Catholic faith, he was required to believe in heaven and hell and a day of judgment. But that was faith and Sebastian wanted more. He had doubts and wished he could be certain of that. He did not want to go by blind faith but belief based on fact. There were still many things about religion that did not make sense to him. Now that he was twenty-four and had been to church a few times, more and more questions were bothering him. Why were priests not allowed to marry, why one man had to die for everybody's sin, why the suffering and why there were so many religions disputing and claiming to be right, yet they believed in the same god? Then there was the clergy, the bishops and the cardinals. They all seemed wealthy yet collected donations at the church. He wondered what they really did with all the money. After all, based on history, Jesus was a simple man without much worldly possessions, and he had always said that his kingdom was not of this world.

Sebastian had an unyielding passion for finding the truth. He desperately wanted to know the workings of the universe and his surroundings and who was behind their design, if anyone. If there was a creator, he wanted to know why religion had been made so complex and ripe with conflicts that had resulted in war and bloodshed.

Gracie half-turned as Sebastian entered the kitchen. She was so proud to see her nephew impeccably dressed this morning in a crisp striped dark grey suit and polka dot black silk tie contrasted against a white linen shirt. He was wearing the pointed Givenchy Oxfords Gracie had given him for his birthday.

"What's for breakfast Gracie," he announced as he came up from behind and kissed her on the forehead. "I am in a hurry." Gracie replied, "Yes, you have that job interview at the studio.

You better get going soon. The scrambled eggs, toast and tea will be a minute. Why don't you get started on the orange juice. Would you like me to make you a sandwich? I have corned beef and rye bread," Aunt Grace suggested, knowing how much Sebastian loved her corned beef sandwich.

"No, Gracie. I shouldn't be too long, probably back by 2:30 latest," he said as he finished his orange juice and started on the scrambled eggs. "I'll grab something on the way back if I am hungry."

"Well, don't fill yourself up. I am making Marsala Chicken Florentine with garlic mashed potatoes for dinner."

"Thanks Gracie". With his mouth salivating at the news of the succulent dinner awaiting him that night, Sebastian got up, buttoned his jacket and prepared to leave.

Aunt Grace could see Sebastian was anxious. Her nephew had been trying to get an interview for two months now, and this was the first one in his field. After graduating at the top of his class at the Film Writers Institute of America, Sebastian had tried unsuccessfully to find a suitable position. He wanted to be independent and support himself. Although he loved Gracie more than anything, he knew he had to start a life of his own.

During the summer of 2014, while he was working a temp job, he had met a very pretty young lady on the bus by the name of Melinda Watkins. She was ever so sweet, caring and soft spoken, and always dressed immaculately that he really liked her. They had talked a few times, but before Sebastian could muster the courage to ask her out on a date, she suddenly disappeared. Could it be something he did or said? Did he come on too strong? Perhaps there was someone else in her life. These thoughts plagued him incessantly for a long time. With fading hope, he had waited day after day hoping to see her board the bus once more. If he only knew where she lived. He wondered what happened to her, and wished he could find someone like her to share his life with. Every time he thought of her his eyes teared up, so he would try very hard not to.

After a quick hug and goodbye to Gracie, Sebastian headed out the door, down the elevator and into the parking lot towards his car. As he slid his six foot one inch frame into the sleek silver grey Acura, his mind was racing. Just two days ago, one of his professors, Jeremy Goldstein, had called him and told him to go see a good friend of his, Jim Stone of Pinnacle Studios who needed someone to find good stories that could possibly be turned into a movie. Sebastian had called Jim and set up a meeting for 9:30 that morning. Jeremy had a very good opinion of Sebastian, and he knew that Jim would provide feedback to Jeremy. He had to impress Jim not only for Jeremy's sake but he really wanted this job. He knew that he was nervous, but he also knew that the way to get rid of the nervousness was to dwell on his past accomplishments and build confidence, remind himself that he was smart, capable and hard working. Then he had to project this in a convincing manner. Images of his graduation ceremony, the standing ovation he received after his Valedictorian speech, 'Adversity: a necessary step towards success' and the admiration of his peers served to boost his morale. Thanks to Gracie who had taught him well, he knew he had the virtues of integrity, loyalty and dedication to offer as well as good working habits and getting along with people.

CHAPTER EIGHT

SEBASTIAN EASED HIS FOOT ON THE ACCELERATOR and merged onto US 101 as he headed towards Hollywood Hills. Rush hour traffic had altogether disappeared by the time he got on the highway, and he set cruise control on the Acura to 75 mph. Now he had some time to think. He had prepared for the interview the best he could, digging into the history of Pinnacle Studios at the local library and on the internet. But he had very little information about Jim Stone, the Vice President of Operations and the person he was soon going to meet.

Over the phone, Simon recalled that Jim was brief and to the point. There were few pleasantries exchanged. It was a simple "Yes, I would like to see you, can you come in at 9:30 AM" when Sebastian had introduced himself and stated that Jeremy Goldstein had suggested that he call Jim. Sebastian knew that Pinnacle had been in business seventeen years and had produced four good movies. But the last one was over three years ago, and there was a rumour circulating that if they did not come up with something in the next six months, they could be in financial trouble.

Sebastian's thoughts again wandered back to his graduation from the Film Writers Institute of America. He had secured the highest mark of his graduating class. He remembered the clapping and photos taken when he stepped onto the podium to accept his degree and how he had wished that his parents had been there. His professors had been very helpful and encouraging during his employment search, but he had been looking for a suitable job for almost two months.

As he pulled into the parking lot of Pinnacle studios, Sebastian turned his attention to the matter at hand. There were three things he had learned that an employer looked for during an interview: can you do the job, are you willing to do the job and will you fit into the organization. He had planned to structure his responses around these specific questions. Then there was always the question, 'what are your weaknesses', which many candidates had trouble answering.

A short distance away, huddled in his small but impressively decorated office, Jim Stone was reviewing Sebastian's resume. He had climbed the ladder the hard way rising through the ranks after having first started as an assistant to the set construction foreman. He had in-depth knowledge of the industry and what was required to make the movie studio successful. The importance of acquiring the right people for key jobs could not be underestimated.

One of the reasons for Jim's success was that he was a stickler for the system. He knew movie stars, producers, politicians and was good friends with the governor. He would take and return favours. There was nothing wrong when both parties benefited. It had been a difficult time for Jim. Due to the financial situation at work he had to take a cut in salary. He was putting in a lot of overtime and had neglected his family. His teenage daughter had a drug problem, and his marriage was falling apart. The increased stress was taking a toll on him. He had also become very short tempered towards his family and even started showing violent behaviour when trying to discipline his daughter. At times he felt like strangling her. A lot was riding on how quickly he could turn things around for the company and himself. The first step was to find a good story that could be turned into a movie. Time was running out, and he did not know how long he could continue like this. Would he crack under the pressure and lose it? He was getting a bit desperate, but he could not show that. Not to the potential job candidate that was about to be introduced to him.

Jim Stone looked up as the well-dressed young man in a distinctive Tom Ford suit was ushered into his office. He quickly stood up and greeted Sebastian with a firm handshake and a cordial but formal smile.

"Good to see you young man. Glad you could come. Please have a seat." Sebastian looked at the two overstuffed brown leather chairs in front of the big wooden desk and sat down on the one closest to him. He looked around and saw that he was surrounded by rosewood panels decorated with pictures of Jim with movie stars, producers and directors. Across from Jim and directly behind him hung a massive TV screen that provided a view into the production floor. From time to time, the frame would switch over to playing excerpts of movies that Pinnacle had produced.

Jim Stone pushed his employees hard, and he expected the best from them. It was a very competitive industry and times were tough. To be successful one had to hit the ground running. Without creativity, hard work and ambition, one could not possibly succeed. He wondered if the young man who had just entered his office would be up to the challenge.

"Your resume looks good academically, but I see you are very short on experience," Jim started out, getting straight to the point. "However what we need is some fresh talent with lots of ideas and willing to work hard. Someone who cannot do this will be out very fast."

"Well, sir, I work hard and smart, and give it everything I've got. I also get along well with people."

"I know, I know," Jim interrupted him impatiently, "and that is why you are here. Jeremy and I go back a long time, and I trust his judgement, and when he recommended you I wanted to see you.

Let me tell you about Pinnacle. We are one of the small, private independent studios. The major studios are doing less and less movies on their own and contracting us to do the production. We also make our own movies, and we rent out stage and production facilities to others.

Things are tough for the industry at this time. At one time movies on the silver screen were one of the only means of entertainment, but as you know times have changed. We now have video games that the younger generation is more involved in. And with cable companies showing more movies on television, even the video rental companies like Blockbuster have gone under. People have big screen televisions at home, or they simply watch movies on Netflix or YouTube on their smart phones. All this cuts into the box office revenue. Rather than depend on others to provide revenue, we want to focus more on making our own movies," he continued.

"Yes, I know there were some good movies from Pinnacle, but I have not seen one for a while now," said Sebastian. "Exactly," replied Jim, "but first we need a good story, a story that will give us a much better chance of success. A lot of the success of a movie lies in the story, and investors are concerned about return on investment, and they want a high degree of confidence that the movie will succeed. They are willing to pay more for it. That is what we need you to do," continued Jim. "We have stories that have to be reviewed for ideas, improvement opportunities and practicality - how we can turn them into scripts and eventually a movie. Better than writing our own story. And that is where you would come in. There are some 15000 stories copyrighted with the Writers Guild every year. Only 700 of them are chosen for movies. Are you aware of green lighting techniques," Jim asked. "It is essential to weed out the good stories from the not so good stories."

Sebastian sensed the chance to make Jim aware of his knowledge in this area. "Certainly. Do you still rely on the age old process of hiring readers to review them because that would be a lot of work?"

Jim's eyes lit up for just a second, enough for Sebastian to realize he had made a hit with the older, seasoned man. "Unfortunately, that is exactly what we have been doing," replied Jim. "It is time consuming and not very productive. Not only do we have disagreements between the readers themselves but also between them and the directors and producers. Yes, we do have experienced readers with acumen, but we have not had much success. That is why we are looking for fresh talent and new ideas."

Jim Stone continued, "The story has to sell not just to the public but also to the directors and producers first. Then it has to attract the big name actors. This will help bring in the investors. Whether it is romance, or adventure or mystery, there has to be twists and turns and surprises. It has to create sympathy for the hero and dislike for the villain. The audience wants to see the hero surpass his or her own abilities and bring out that inner strength. They want to see the flaws and how he or she overcomes them."

Jim was quiet for a moment expecting Sebastian to take this in. Sebastian felt he had to add something to show he understood and agreed with Jim.

"And then there has to be conflict, internal within the hero and with the villain. The audience does not have to like the hero or villain but understand what they are doing and why."

Jim did not say anything but smiled approvingly. This was the cue Sebastian was waiting for. He sensed the opportunity to move forward and impress Jim Stone even further.

"Yes we certainly can use some objective methodology to select those stories that will cut down on the human review and disagreements. I realize picking a good story is like picking a good horse before a race."

"What do you have in mind," Jim asked.

"What we want to do is to look at the scripts of successful movies and find a correlation between the story's words and the success of the movie," replied Sebastian.

"But we do not have access to electronic forms of movie scripts," questioned Jim.

Sebastian nodded. "That is true but we have spoilers - these are between four and twenty page summaries of the movie's story written by people who give you the essence of the movie before you watch it, hence the name spoilers. Then we do a word-bag of the spoiler, which is essentially a count of certain words. There is more to a story than just frequencies of certain words. Besides, there are ways to tell a story. 'Hero kills villain' and 'villain kills hero' would have the same word-bag, but the latter would not be appealing to an audience. Then there are multiple scenes and unexpected endings with an emotional touch that cannot be measured by words alone."

"How do you propose we handle that?" Jim enquired.

"I am not saying we eliminate human judges completely. We would have to supplement the automated textual analysis with the human factor to pickup genre and content information. Readers would become reviewers and would also compare the results with a list of preset questions that would help the prediction model."

"Questions such as . . ." Jim Stone was now leaning forward his eyes showing great interest in what Sebastian was saying.

"The story follows a logical, causal relationship. Coincidences are avoided. Each scene description advances the plot and is closely connected to the central conflict. The story contains elements of surprise but is logical within context and within its own rules. We want to keep readers trying to anticipate what would happen next. Even though the ending is logical and believable, it must carry surprise and is unexpected."

Jim Stone knew very well what made a great story and what characteristics it had to have, but he wanted to hear Sebastian say that. He smiled broadly and stood up. "Sebastian, I believe we need someone like you, so when can you start?"

Sebastian was surprised at the abruptness of the offer but quickly replied, "When would you like me to start?"

CHAPTER NINE

MONDAY MORNING AT 7:30 A.M., SEBASTIAN TURNED his silver Acura into the parking lot of Pinnacle Movie Studios and parked besides a vintage pearl white 1963 Oldsmobile convertible. It was his first day at the new job. He inspected the beauty and wondered who owned the car. The car had looked huge from the outside, but when Sebastian peeked in through the window, he was greeted to a massive interior. Enormous red leather seats that looked more like couches. Dark wood paneling with intricate design and a steering wheel with the Oldsmobile logo accented the analog speedometer dial and gearbox. He wondered how it would feel to drive. Probably like a boat, he thought.

His thoughts once again started to race. He had to make a plan and stick to it. First, he thought of checking scripts with the Writers Guild. It was the easy way out and he could probably find some good stories. But then he figured, why spend time and money only to realize that someone else has probably decided on the story. Good stories don't sit around for long. It was a gamble. He would first go through stories directly mailed in, and see if there were any that were not up for public access through Writers Guild. But most scripts were registered with Writers Guild first for copyright purposes.

Sebastian also thought about writing a story, something original. That would take a lot of time and even though he was good at writing, he was not sure he could pull it off. "As a last resort," he muttered to himself, "if I have no other choice."

The petite, attractive redhead at the reception desk smiled as Sebastian walked in the front doors.

"You must be Sebastian, the new story writer. I'm Tina, Tina Reeves," she said, adjusting the black headband she was wearing.

Sebastian walked over to the reception and smiled back. "I am very pleased to meet you."

Tina's light brown eyes lit up as she smiled again and said, "Let me show you to your office."

She was immaculately dressed in beige slacks, a royal blue jacket and white frilled shirt, all neatly pressed. Sebastian could sense the aroma of the Dior J'adore perfume with its titillating sensual fragrance of Arabian jasmine mixed with Damask rose. As he followed her, they went down a short corridor where there were two signs. One sign read 'Studio City' and the other 'Administrative Offices.' They headed down the corridor, past rooms on either side. The rooms had small windows to the corridor but Sebastian hardly looked anywhere except at Tina who was a couple of feet ahead of him. She seemed to have a great personality and in her mid-twenties. Perhaps he could take her out for coffee and get to know her better, he thought. His heart was beating hard and he desperately wanted to start a conversation with her but did not know how. He quickly realized his mistake as Tina abruptly slowed down and opened the door at the end of the corridor. As she held the door open, he noticed that she had a wedding band on her finger.

Sebastian felt his heart drop suddenly. This girl was supremely beautiful and a class act. *Dang! All the good ones are taken*, he said to himself.

"Here's the room you will be working in," Tina said. "And make yourself comfortable. If there is anything you need just dial 0 for the reception, and I will put you in touch with the right person," she continued with an air of confidence. Sebastian thanked her and did not let his disappointment show.

Wow, he thought, *they put the reins in my hand right away.*

Hands on learning. I suppose that is the best way.

He decided to roll up his sleeves and get to work immediately. Looking around he saw a clean desk with only a pile of paper and a folder. The folder contained telephone number extensions for different departments and names of executives. His name was not there.

He thought, *I hope this is not a temporary job.*

He made a note to ask Jim why his name was not there. Perhaps they did not have time to update the list, but he had accepted the job over a week ago.

The office was very modest with plain veneer paneling on three sides and two windows. One looked out into the corridor, the other on the opposite side onto the parking lot. He could see a short, bald man in his fifties get into the Oldsmobile and drive away. *I wonder if that is the president of the studio*, thought Sebastian.

There was a bookshelf on one side. Sebastian started browsing the titles. They all had to do with story writing, Writers Guild rules, self-help for novelists for turning scripts into movies. Although he knew quite a bit already, this would be a handy reference if he ever needed one.

Sebastian decided he would get a cup of coffee and start going through the pile of paper on his desk to see if there was anything useful for him. He had not seen a coffee machine in the reception area or corridor, so he decided to call Tina.

"Tina, where do I get a cup of coffee? I did not see a coffee machine. Is there a common area or lunch room where I could get coffee?"

"Tell me what kind of coffee you like, and I will bring it to you," she replied.

This seemed strange but great. Coffee delivered to the office. He chuckled and thought, *I wonder if lunch is delivered too.* "Just plain coffee, double cream no sugar, and piping hot"

A few minutes later, Tina knocked on his door with the coffee, and to Sebastian's amazement asked what he wanted for lunch and when he would like it delivered. He was speechless. *Was every employee treated this way, or was he special?*

"A roast beef sub would be fine, I noticed a Subway down the street. Actually I can go get it myself," he said trying to calm the nervousness in his voice.

Why was he feeling this way around Tina? He could just feel a lot of chemistry between them.

"That won't be necessary because I was going to go pickup food for a bunch of other people, and I can get some for you," replied Tina with a smile.

A few minutes passed by and Sebastian settled down. He had gulped down some coffee and now was taking sips as he started turning the pages of what looked like stories for review. There were about 60 scripts. Luckily, they were short, concise summaries of about 75 pages each. That was still about 4500 pages that he had to go through.

* * * *

Two weeks had gone by and Sebastian had gone through little more than half the pile. Every day the coffee came, and the lunch came and yet his name was not on the directory. Just Tina's cherubic face beaming at him every time the door opened. He was very attracted to her, and this was not going to be easy. Nobody else had called him or come to the door. He had not seen Jim. It was simply in to work, saying Hi to Tina and going into his office. He would bury himself in reviewing stories, get his coffee and lunch, and at the end of the day leave, saying goodbye to Tina. He wanted to distance himself from her and at the same time wanted to be close to her. Their eyes would frequently meet. She was friendly, but she was also married, and he knew better. For the time being he decided to just be courteous and greet her. Somehow he had the uncomfortable feeling that she liked him. That would be great except she has a husband, he figured.

There were only six scripts that Sebastian really liked, so he started to review each one of them in detail.

The first script talked about an alien invasion of earth. Yes, there were a lot of movies of aliens invading the planet, but this one had a unique twist. The aliens knew that they were being monitored by earthlings, and their invasion strategy was based around this knowledge. The humans came up with all these elaborate plans to defeat the aliens but were outsmarted every time. They finally realized that the aliens were monitoring their every move and devised a way to lead them on. In the end, it was a battle of wits and courage that saved the human race.

Another story was a sad romantic tale. A regular boy-meets-girl, boy likes girl and pursues her and sends her a love poem. She replies but it ends up being deleted from his email without him ever seeing it. He moves away and gets married, and she unknowingly seeks him only to find out the sad truth about the deleted email. The boy then has to deal with a lot of mixed emotions and ends up having to make a very difficult choice to be with her or his wife and kids.

Yet another story was about a poor boy who has an accident and goes into a coma. In the coma he dreams about living in a big house on a ranch with horses and cattle and a lot of expensive things. Meanwhile, his family does get rich and does buy a big house on a ranch with horses and cattle and other things that were in his dream. When the boy comes out of the coma, he has to deal with a lot of situations where he does not know what is real and what is from his dream.

Then there was a clash of two super heroes who had both been hypnotised and made evil.

Hmm, interesting but people don't want to see their superheroes as evil, Sebastian thought.

The fifth story was about virtual wars replacing conventional battles. Mankind had reached a stage of evolution where they realized that there was only destruction with wars, yet wars could not be discarded totally because there were genuine grievances, land claims and greed for territorial expansion. So it was decided that each country's arsenal would be verified and put into a super computer, which would then fight the battle so as to give an accurate outcome. Based on the result, the losing country would actually have to surrender resources that the computer decided went to the victor. If they did not, the victor would have the right to start an actual war ending with the predicted results - but it would never come to that. This way, while the victor grabbed the spoils of war, there would be no life lost nor any destruction.

Finally there was a comedy about a naive student who starts a political party called Open Policy. The platform is about coming totally clean to the constituents by having all revenues, expenses and budgets made available to people in electronic form with drill down enquiries to the original documents for verification. One could see all competing bids and tenders, legitimate expenditures and expose any under-the-table transactions so bribery and corruption was eliminated. The only problem was that even though he became immensely popular, he could not find any honest candidates. So he had to resort to back room deals and bribes to win over staff and candidates to run for election. It was tough on his conscience as he realized he had to play the dirty game of politics.

Sebastian had almost finished the last of the six scripts he had set aside when he heard a knock on the door. Before he could get up the door opened a little and Jim Stone peeked in.

"Hello Sebastian, are you busy? Can I come in?"

"Of course. I have not seen you . . .," responded Sebastian.

Before he could finish, Jim had already walked in and sat in the chair in front of Sebastian's desk.

"How have things been going in the last couple of weeks?" "Actually quite well," replied Sebastian, a bit surprised that Jim had gotten so quickly to the point. "I have been reading a lot of stories and applying a kind of quick judgment to what should be moved ahead. After additional review on these, I then selected six stories for detailed analysis and possible green-lighting techniques. Should get back to you within a week on a quality story that we could convert into a movie script and move forward with."

"Have you checked them with Writers Guild to know who they belong to? We also would want to contact them as soon as possible and discuss the financial terms."

"No, but I will. Hopefully one of them will come through for us."

"Good," replied Jim.

Sebastian could not wait to ask Jim, "I noticed that my name is not on the directory."

He was about to continue and dying to ask if the job was permanent when Jim replied, "That is because I do not want anyone to disturb you. You see we are in a time crunch, and desperately need to find and get moving on a good story, and your job is critical. And that is why we don't even want you to spend time going out for lunch or to get coffee."

Sebastian was astounded. Jim had certainly thought of everything, from giving Sebastian the office at the end of the hallway to not disturbing him or allowing distractions. He was all business and Sebastian understood why.

CHAPTER TEN

IT WAS EARLY TUESDAY AFTERNOON AND SEBASTIAN had been working hard on preparing his submission on the six scripts to present to Jim. He had compared them to similar scripts - turned-to-movies and measured their success and had also created some possibly different outcomes for the stories. These stories had been turned from mere words to a draft movie script with some scenes, camera angles, dialogues, characters. There were heroes and villains, emotions, twists and turns and even a bit of mystery. He was quite satisfied that Jim would be impressed with these and be able to make a choice. However all six had been registered with Writers Guild and were accessible to other movie studios. He felt they were ready for advanced green lighting and to work out a cost and a return on investment for possible investors.

Sebastian badly needed a break. He had been working intensely and was focussed on getting to this stage, but it had taken a toll on him. He had to take a break before the big moment of presenting them to Jim. He prayed that Jim would not strike down or criticize his work. Sebastian's fears got the better of him. What if he got fired?

It had taken him several months to find a job he liked and it would be disastrous to get fired from his first full time job.

Then there was Tina. He was developing feelings for her, feelings he was trying hard to control. He badly needed to get his mind off the pressure and decided to take a walk down Studio City.

Sebastian opened the black frosted glass door with the words 'Studio City' written in white and saw a long corridor with offices on both sides. Signs prominently displayed the areas he passed. The offices were grouped by pre-production, production and post-production stages. Within each group, doors opened into offices that were part of that group.

There was a bespectacled, silver haired gentleman in a dark blue suit coming out of one of the doors Sebastian passed. A sense of relief overcame Sebastian. *Yes, someone else did work here besides Jim and Tina.*

"Hi, my name is Sebastian, script reviewer. Glad to meet you." "Arthur Davirro, production accountant," replied Arthur in a soft spoken, cultivated low key voice.

"You must be the numbers guy?"

"Yes, I am in charge of all the budgets and expenses. All proposals come to me and then I advise Jim on which ones are viable from a fiscal view point."

"I just started a short while ago. What about you?" "Been here almost six years."

"I am heading out to Studio City. Would you like to join me?" "Would love too, but I have to head home. Son's eighteenth birthday and we are having a lot of his young friends over for a party."

"Well, see you later."

"Sure thing. Enjoy your visit. It is quite something in there" Arthur said, pointing down the corridor.

As he neared the end of corridor, he saw a grey steel door ahead, and a table with hard hats and safety goggles to the left of the door. The security guard by the door handed these to him and after he had worn the hat and glasses, he was allowed through into the actual production area.

As he stepped into the production area, Sebastian was taken aback by its sheer size. He knew there was a lot of complexity in a movie studio, but this was something else. It was like a giant warehouse with 40 foot ceilings. There were actually five warehouses joined together each in excess of one hundred thousand square feet. Several walkways criss-crossed and looked like intersections, with streets having their own name. At times there were two lanes, even a roundabout for the forklifts coming and going to the area where the sets were located. Construction seemed to be the main visible activity with some sets being prepared and others being pulled down.

Out of nowhere a short bald man in his fifties approached Sebastian. "I am the manager, Cecil Morrison. Haven't seen you before. You must be new here."

At once Sebastian recognized him as the owner of the Oldsmobile in the parking lot. "Just started about two weeks ago"

"How can I help you?" the bald man asked politely, wiping his forehead. Sebastian could see Cecil had a lot on his mind and did not really want to spend too much time with him.

"I'm just going to look around. Get a feel for how this operation is really run. You have a beautiful old classic out there. Could not help admiring her."

"Thank you. Go ahead, look around. You will find it quite interesting." Cecil had hardly finished speaking as he turned and headed away between a row of shelves to the left.

There was a main walkway that seemed to stretch ahead for a mile or so it seemed. Sebastian did not want to spend too much time here because he did not want Jim to think he was wandering off, so he walked briskly. The landscape around him seemed to change every few minutes. There were the fully done up sets, which felt like he was walking through a Rooms To Go store. The next area, of partially completed sets looked like a sub division under construction. Some rooms he could not even see into. They only had a door. These were the sound stages isolated from outside noise. After that, he saw an area that looked more like a Home Depot, with shelves of hardware supplies. light fixtures, electric cable and camera equipment.

Beautiful costumes hung on racks stretching hundreds of feet ahead of him. There were dresses, gowns, suits and tuxedos, medieval clothes and even suits of armour. Suddenly Sebastian could smell fragrances and knew he was approaching the makeup, cosmetics and hair dressing area. Sebastian glanced at his GuTe watch. He had been walking for a good fifteen minutes and was so fascinated and intrigued with what was going on around him that he had not noticed the time. By now he had almost reached the end and was in the receiving department where trucks were unloading supplies and equipment

As he began to turn around and hasten back, he saw a small half-open door with a bluish green light emanating from it. The sign on it 'Archived tapes' raised his curiosity. Sebastian hesitated then muttered to himself, "What the heck. I have come this far. A couple of extra minutes won't make any difference." He stepped inside.

There were rows of film tape on shelves stacked from the ground to the ceiling. Reels and reels of unedited film.

"Not much to see here," he exclaimed.

About to leave, he spotted a stack of papers on a table against the left wall. They appeared to be discarded stories, with a half page summary followed by a reason for rejection. A bold red REJECTION stamp, at a forty-five degree angle appeared on the top page of each summary.

Sebastian sat down and quickly began browsing a few stories because he wanted to know the reason for their rejection. Perhaps he could apply some of the criteria for rejection to the stories he was reading. The stories were old and dusty and the paper they were written on was starting to turn yellow and get brittle. He quickened his pace and tried some speedreading, turning over the stories quickly.

Then he saw it, and it stuck out like a sore thumb. He had gotten about two thirds through the pile, and turned it over only to see a script with no summary, no rejection and no dust!

Had this been missed? And why did it have no dust on it when it was surrounded by dust? The paper had a very light bluish green hue to it. Seemed mysterious, almost ominous.

Time had gone by faster than he had thought, so Sebastian decided that he would head home. He folded and tucked the mysterious script in his inside coat pocket and headed back. *Might make for some good reading over the weekend, and I'm sure no one is going to miss it.*

What was supposed to be a weekend of relaxed reading and enjoyment turned into shock and awe and three sleepless nights. As he read more of the script he became more immersed in it, and it seemed to consume him. Sebastian did not even bother to look for the author of the script. He was getting answers to all his questions as a child, like the creation of the universe, the purpose behind our existence and why there was so much chaos and misery in the world around him.

Every few minutes he would exclaim, "Oh my God!" His brain was racing at a feverish pace trying to sort out all the information that it was receiving and all the sense this script was making. Every time he would think of a question, the answer would be right there as he read on. It seemed the words of the script, his brain and some supernatural source were all connected and working together,

A mathematically coded document brought by the messenger of the covenant with solutions to our most pressing problems, he thought as he reviewed the criminal justice system proposed by the story. *This will eliminate the expensive prison system. A moral code and economic system. And yes, killing the murderer does not bring the victim back, only makes his dependants and the dependants of the victim consume tax payer money. It all makes so much sense.*

What Sebastian read next brought tears to his eyes. The script talked about the age of responsibility. Sebastian had always wondered at what age the human being would be held responsible. His own Catholic faith had put the age at Twelve. He knew the punishment had to fit the crime, and it seemed most unlikely to him that a merciful creator would condemn a twelve year old to eternal damnation no matter how bad he or she was. Life was full of distractions. People had to get an education, a job, and find someone to get married to and settle down with a family before they could really ponder the more philosophical aspects of life. The phrases 'Life begins at forty' and 'Everything until forty is just rehearsal' came to his mind.

"Omigosh!" he exclaimed, suddenly realizing about his parents. "They died at the age of thirty-eight. The good die young."

And it explained so much. Now he had an answer to why the children died and how blessed they were. He knew where his parents had gone, and he felt comforted by it. The tears rolling down his cheeks were tears of joy.

Sebastian then did something very interesting. He took a piece of paper and jotted down all the questions he had as a child. Questions such as why were there so many stars, why were they so far away, did anybody live there and where did they come from? He then added more questions that had bothered him as he turned into an adult. Is there a Creator, a Designer or did all this come together by itself? What is the purpose of life? What function, if any, do the animals serve? Why are we the only creatures with free will and ability to reason? While he was fascinated with science for shedding light on a lot of the hows behind the working of things, he also felt disappointed that it could never answer the whys behind it. Here all the whys were being answered.

Then he read the script again, and every time one of his questions from the sheet of paper was answered, he crossed it out. Before he realized it, he had been through the script and all his questions had been crossed out.

A mathematically coded document providing the first scientific proof for the existence of God! A document that could provide answers to our most urgent questions and solutions to our most pressing problems! He had always disputed the biblical version that we were all here because Adam and Eve had disobeyed God. And a loving God would not allow His creation to suffer wars, chaos, misery and disease. This script was answering all these issues satisfactorily, and it made perfect sense. Wow!

"This could change the world. This will change the world," he shouted out in the middle of the night. Had Gracie not been sleeping with ear plugs in the adjoining bedroom, he would have surely awakened her. The advent of certainty would change the whole equation. There would be no need for blind faith anymore. The battle between creationists and evolutionists would end forever.

If the existence of God were to be proved, a new sense of awe would descend on the world and a focussed attempt to do right, knowing that we were being watched and would be judged.

He pondered whether he should tell Gracie. Maybe it was premature. Perhaps she was too steeped in her beliefs. Sebastian knew that people held whatever religious beliefs they had as sacred, and it was just a no-no to talk to people about religion. All he knew was that she believed in God and had very strong faith in Him. It was better to leave it for now. After all, she would only be held responsible for what she knew. No point burdening her more than necessary.

Sebastian had been so busy reading the story that he had forgotten all about the author. Quickly he turned to the last page. To his amazement there was no author listed, no contact number or address. Then he noticed it. At the bottom of the last page, in the middle were a bunch of what looked like golden apples. He counted them. There were seven.

Certain things in the story had raised his eyebrow. The seven apples had heightened his curiosity even more. He had heard of the Spirit of Truth being quoted. There was a reference to a mathematically coded document as being the first scientific proof of the existence of God, and the part about a Messenger of the Covenant. What covenant was this? Was it the one God made with Abraham, or with the Children of Israel? Or was it some other covenant? As if this was not enough, there was an unambiguous reference to a date when the world would end in both solar and lunar years. *How ingenious*, he thought. *If a number of years to the end of the world were given, there would be a dispute whether they were solar years or lunar years. But this made it very clear.*

As sensational as it sounded, Sebastian knew that predictions about the end of the world were many, and all of them wrong, and to even attempt to mention this would make him lose all credibility. He decided to remove this completely from his mind.

Now, he decided to investigate further. He would need time, lots of time. The key was to find the author of the story, but all he had to work with was seven golden apples.

Suddenly he thought of his work, and the deadline and meeting with Jim on Monday afternoon. This story was too important to ignore. He had to delay Jim until he could figure out how to present this to him and talk him into turning it into a movie.

CHAPTER ELEVEN

WALKING AT A BRISK PACE, SEBASTIAN MADE HIS way along the long corridor to Jim Stone's office. Flashes came back of the brief conversation he had with Jim the week before. How he had asked for an extension and how he had been denied one. Jim had made it very clear that time was of the essence, and he could not wait any longer to see something. Sebastian also felt a bit of weakness in his knees, not just because of the anxiety but also because he had been up all night preparing for something to present to Jim. After a long debate within himself, he had finally decided to tell Jim that this script was more important than the six others he had picked out.

All Jim knew was there was a really dramatic story Sebastian had found, and it had a very unique twist to it. He had reluctantly agreed to spend fifteen minutes with Sebastian before his busy day began. As Sebastian opened the door of Jim's office and greeted him with a smile, Jim looked up expectantly and with a hint of irritation. He was wondering if Sebastian's youth and inexperience had gotten the better of him.

Jim got straight to the point.

"You seemed very excited about this story you apparently found in the archives. Those are all rejected stories, only to be used for reference purposes."

Sebastian started to explain how the story he found did not have any rejection stamp, no dust, and no author and how it dealt with subjects of interest to the curious mind wanting to know the purpose of life and answers to many of the problems plaguing society. He touched on an apparent divine mathematical code in a document coded beyond human ability. Just when Sebastian thought he had Jim's interest, Jim cut him off sharply. "Dammit, this has to do with religion. We are not making a religious documentary. That is out of the question. Even if we were, it would be based on history, not on a fictional story of numbers and philosophy. We are making a movie, for God's sake. Let's get real."

Sebastian was taken aback but still adamant. "We could make it in such a way that there would be subliminal messages that could leave people wondering, and tell their family and friends, and this would potentially make the audience huge, especially since it was geared towards the idea of an alien message and would appeal to the younger generation and kids."

Jim thought that over. "I know a movie with religious overtones is risky. Everyone believes in whatever they do and think they are right. This is going to upset many people especially if you present it as truth. Besides, you don't even know the author.

Find the author and get me something that I can really present..."

"What do you mean when you say *really present?*" enquired Sebastian

Jim replied, "I mean . . . well, a smoking gun. Something that will give the audience enough interest to pardon us for doing a religious movie."

"Okay. But all I ask for is some time. There is research to do, and I have to talk to people and get answers. I need a couple of months."

Jim said nothing. Sebastian smiled to himself. Jim did not say no. He had gotten a concession from Jim. That is all he wanted. Now he had the time to do his research, find the author and rework the story into a meaningful script. He thanked Jim and got up to leave

"Remember, I can only give you four weeks tops." were the last words he heard as he closed the door of Jim's office and walked out.

* * * *

Sebastian knew his time was limited, so he got down to business. His primary objective was to first find the author of the mysterious story. As intriguing as the seven apples at the end of the story seemed, it was really nothing to work with. He figured he first had to find out about other religions. Even though his parents grew up as Catholics, religion was not a part of their life, and they were largely secular. They were good people, and they believed in a supernatural being, who created the earth and the surrounding universe with its stars. There was never any talk of other sects of Christianity, let alone other religions.

He would make his plan. First, he would investigate all the major religions by getting hold of their scriptures or other literature and books to see if he could find out any prophesies about a person coming that would give us all the answers. Perhaps it was Jesus, or Muhammad the prophet of Islam that came after him. Or maybe it was someone before Jesus, like Abraham or Moses. Even Buddha or

Confucius or someone else. Sebastian was determined to find out. He knew with so many religious overtones in the story, the author had to be a religious person.

Or was it God Himself? The very thought of this sent a shiver along his spine. From an early age his mother taught him that God was omniscient and knew all the wrong things we did. We were all under His ever-watchful eye.

That evening Sebastian sat in his bedroom surrounded by books. Gracie had noticed her young nephew was acting a bit strange over the past three weeks, quite reserved and deep in thought, and she gave him the space he needed. When she saw the pile of books he brought in, she noticed they were religious books and the thick leather bound version of the King James Bible did not leave a doubt. She figured he was trying to come to grips with his spirituality and find his peace. After all, he had been through a lot, what with his parents dying when he was so young.

Sebastian was very glad that Gracie did not ask or bombard him with questions. He did not know how to answer them, nor did he want to go into the history of what had happened in the last little while. He had a deadline, and he had a job to do, and he had to remain focussed. He did not want to go back to Jim empty handed, only to say he wasted four weeks of precious time. Jim had told him his job was critical, and the future of the studio may well depend on it. He had a huge responsibility on his shoulders.

After three days of reading the Bible, Sebastian realized he had way too much on his plate. He had read Genesis and found out about the story of creation and had continued reading Exodus and started on Leviticus. While he saw answers to the how, he did not see any reasons as to the why. He had hardly covered a hundred Chapters out of eleven hundred and eighty-nine in the whole Bible. There was not just the Old Testament but the New Testament as well. That was only Christianity. He still had the Torah and the Koran to go through as the other monotheistic religions. Then there was the Bhagwad Gita of the Hindus, and the writings of Sikh gurus and teachings of Confucius and Zoroaster. This was not working out as he expected.

He decided to cut short his misstep. Instead, he would go to online versions and search for particular words. He decided to search for the words 'Spirit of Truth', 'Messenger of the Covenant' and 'mathematically coded document.'

Sebastian started making notes. While there were about forty different translations of John 16:13 that came up, they all said the same thing, so he wrote down, "However, when he, the Spirit of truth, is come, he will guide you into all truth: for he shall not speak of himself; but whatever he shall hear, that shall he speak: and he will tell you things to come."

It seemed that Christians universally agreed that the messenger of the covenant was Jesus Christ, and the covenant was between God and man that God would send a Redeemer and Saviour. But was this the same as the Spirit of Truth? There were so many unanswered questions, or answers that did not make sense. Would we all be down here on Earth just because Adam and Eve disobeyed God? Why would God allow such events that would lead to the sacrifice of His son? Could His foreknowledge not allow Him to prevent this in the first place? Was God not omniscient?

Another thing that did not make sense to Sebastian was how the Trinity, the concept of three-in-one godhood could be reconciled to the concept of one omnipotent God. There were two other references to the Messenger of the Covenant that he pulled up, which seemed very interesting. One was from the Old Testament and the other from the Koran.

"Behold, I am going to send My messenger, and he will clear the way before Me. And the Lord, whom you seek, will suddenly come to His temple; and the messenger of the covenant, in whom you delight, behold, He is coming," says the LORD of hosts. "But who can endure the day of His coming? And who can stand when He appears? For He is like a refiner's fire and like fullers' soap...." (Malachi 3:1-2)

"GOD took a covenant from the prophets, saying, 'I will give you the scripture and wisdom. Afterwards, a messenger will come to confirm all existing scriptures. You shall believe in him and support him.' He said, 'Do you agree with this, and pledge to fulfill this covenant?' They said, 'We agree.' He said, 'You have thus borne witness, and I bear witness along with you.'" (Koran 3:81)

Sebastian looked at these verses in stunned silence. All the major monotheistic religions were referencing the same individual but from a different perspective. Perhaps they got it all from the same source. Certainly he felt anything coming from God would be consistent and without contradiction.

At the same time, Jews did not believe in Jesus at all. They actually saw him as a fraudster and blasphemer who claimed that God had a son, and someone who preached that he was that son. So how would they be saved? Then what about Muslims who thought about Jesus as a prophet sent by God, and Buddhists, Hindus and all others who did not even believe in Jesus at all.

He found a beautiful verse in the Bhagwad Gita, "Let us meditate on God, His glorious attributes, who is the basis of everything in this universe as its Creator, who is fit to be worshiped as Omnipresent, Omnipotent, Omniscient, and self existent conscious being, who removes all ignorance and impurities from the mind and purifies and sharpens our intellect"

[Gayatri Mantra, Yajur Veda]

Surely someone who believed in the above would not be outside God's grace and mercy, thought Sebastian. All these questions were bothering Sebastian, but he kept reminding himself that the answers would come, but first he had to find out who the author of the script was.

Sebastian decided he was going to meet with a religious scholar from each of the three major monotheistic religions and query them about the messenger of the covenant. Meanwhile, he was going to study all the references about the messenger of the covenant. This would take a while and he decided it was so important that he would have to miss his deadline with Jim Stone. Nevertheless, it was something he had to do, and he would pursue it for as long as it took. The information from the hidden script was so powerful and with such momentous implications that it contradicted all established principles of the major religions.

Or did it really? Sebastian asked himself. The founders of all these religions had preached the worship of the One True God, yet the teachings preached today were in stark contrast to those very original fundamentals, it seemed. Instead of peace, there was war. Instead of tolerance, there was bigotry, and compassion was replaced by greed and selfishness.

He simply had to get to the bottom of all this.

And for this, he would travel to the Holy Land where it all originated, Jerusalem. The next stop would be Rome and the Vatican followed by the prestigious Al-Azhar University in Cairo, the Mecca of learning of Islamic culture, history and religion itself.

CHAPTER TWELVE

AS HE EMBARKED ON HIS JOURNEY, SEBASTIAN thought, *I have a pretty good idea of religions, but I need to ask questions and get answers or clues about the existence of the Messenger of the Covenant.* Clear blue skies greeted Sebastian as the El-Al Airbus descended towards Tel Aviv's Ben Gurion International Airport. Named after David Ben Gurion, Israel's first prime minister, Ben Gurion Airport is the largest airport in Israel and handles about fifteen million passengers a year. It is situated about nineteen kilometres south-east of the City Centre.

As Sebastian emerged from the plane into Terminal 3, there was no escaping the stringent security. Uniformed and plain clothes police and army personnel where stationed throughout. Israelis took the security of their airport very seriously and for good reason. There had been a number of terrorist attempts here.

Sebastian walked between the water fountains towards the high columns of the reception centre before taking the elevators on the left towards Customs. After collecting his luggage, he boarded a sherut, a shared taxi that would take him to Jerusalem.

The sherut wound its way along highway 1, the main corridor that connects the airport with Tel Aviv. It was a great opportunity to take in the sights of the countryside and landscape of Israel. Highway 1 had undergone some major improvements in recent years. Mountains had been carved and curves flattened and a couple of tunnels added to reduce the travel time. Coming out from Tel Aviv Highway 1 curves like an S around Ben Gurion and narrows from a six lane highway to a four lane highway and then rises ninety-three metres at Ben Sherman before slowly making a slight descent, before it again turns south east and travels through the Ayalon Valley.

Sebastian caught a glimpse of the Tel-Aviv Jerusalem High Speed Railway Bridge, the longest bridge in Israel before the sherut again started making an ascent towards Green Line and Sha'ar HaGai (The Valley Gate), three hundred metres above sea level. Near the interchange, on the south side of the highway, Sebastian could see an Ottoman Caravanserai, units arranged around a central courtyard providing amenities for travellers. As they continued to ascend to over seven hundred metres they went past the famous Burma Road, where rusted and abandoned military vehicles lay, a commemoration to the war effort of the Jerusalem Convoys during the War of Independence.

Now the sherut began its final descent towards Jerusalem. The Yellin House Visitors' Center near the municipal limits of Jerusalem lay near the dangerous Motza curve at an elevation of five hundred and sixty metres. Rather than go through Ben Gurion boulevard, the sherut took the interchange at Sha'ar Moriah. Instead of ending up at the historic western entrance of Jerusalem, the sherut descended into the Valley of Cedars, or road number 9. Again, they went through a tunnel on the north side of the Srek Stream and finally ended on the four-lane highway 50. Before he knew it, the sherut pulled up into the Oliver Tree hotel on St. George Street, in the American Colony.

The Olive Tree Hotel is one of Jerusalem's most popular hotels. Most of the front facade is illuminated by green light. The foyer is embellished by a cavern with high ceilings and a big tree that bears a semblance to the burning bush. Interior stone walls have embedded pillars that are lighted from below. Around the tree are wooden tables and chairs. Legend has it that from the garden, you can still hear the sounds of King David's harp to this day, as he serenaded pilgrims.

After a quick check-in Sebastian retired to his room, a well-appointed suite with flat screen TV and internet, and neat brown sofa with black striped orange cushions, and a double bed with orange towel and black borders laid across. *A very cosy room,* he thought. He felt tired after the long day's travel and decided to call room service for dinner. After watching some news on TV, he glanced at his watch and prepared to retire for the night. It was 10:22 pm.

The historic Holy City was only a ten-minute walk away. Sebastian got up bright and early and treated himself to a lavish breakfast of steak and eggs, then embarked on his journey to the Hurva. Soon the Tower of David became visible as he approached the Jaffe Gate, also known as the Gate of David. Most of the gates are built at right angles so as to prevent a battering ram or other aggressive measures by some invading force. Once inside, he passed by the graves of the two architects that were commissioned by Suleiman, the Ottoman King and walked straight to the IDF square, making a right to enter the Jewish Quarter of the Old City. He walked through the Main Square where all alleys lead. It was a bustling Thursday afternoon, and there were a lot of activities and places to get refreshments, so he sat down on a bench and looked towards the Hurva.

The Hurva is one of the most beautiful synagogues in Israel and a very popular tourist destination. It has a white dome and the sides are arched with half-moon windows. Around the lower part of the dome, there is a circular metal railing, which gives a great view of the Jewish Quarter and Tower of David. At night the Hurva is illuminated and basks in a glorious yellowish light.

Hurva means 'ruin' and this monument has a rich history of destruction and rebuilding. Designed in the neo-Byzantine style by the followers of Rabbi Judah, it was completed in 1856. Muslims destroyed it in 1721, and it lay in ruins for 140 years and became known as the Ruin, or Hurva. It was again destroyed by the Arab League in 1948. After the six-day Arab Israeli war, it was rebuilt. Originally there was a high wooden Birmah in the middle and crystal chandeliers hung from the domed ceiling.

Sebastian made his way to Ha-Yehudim Street and opened the metal gate to enter the roman-era cobbled stone courtyard around the Hurva. He took the two set of stairs on the left to the main entrance. What caught Sebastian's attention as he walked in was the Holy Ark on the eastern wall. Flanked by four Corinthian columns, it is built on two levels and surrounded by wooden carvings of birds and flowers. It was imported from the Nikolaijewsky synagogue in Kherson, Russia.

He entered the prayer area through three iron gates and gazed upon the Holy Ark before making his way between the rows of wooden benches on either side towards the reading desk. There were not many people around. An old man, bent forward, was sweeping the floors around the reading desk. A short bearded man wearing black pants, a white shirt and tie, and a kippah, prayer shawl and borsalino hat, who had apparently just finished reading from the Jewish holy writings was getting ready to put away some scrolls. Sebastian approached the short bearded man with an outstretched hand.

"I am Sebastian Girard from Los Angeles. I am looking for the rabbi."

"The Chief Rabbi is not here. I am his assistant Rabbi Moshe Aaron."

"You have a lovely synagogue here, especially the Holy Ark. It is so grand."

"Thank you, Sebastian. How may I help you?"

"I am here to ask some questions about Judaism."

"You came all the way from the United States to find out about Judaism? I used to live in the United States, but the love of our heritage and history and religion brought me back to my roots, the land chosen for us Jews by Yehovah. My dear Sebastian I want to tell you that Judaism is the oldest of the three Abrahamic religions. We are the Children of Israel, the chosen people with whom God made the covenant. You see Israel was Jacob, the grandson of the patriarch Abraham." Moshe looked out of the corner of his eyes and smiled at Sebastian

Sebastian smiled back. "I know. I have studied religion over the past little while and have a great interest in comparative religion."

Moshe continued, "Jews are special people and privileged in this sense. You cannot just become a Jew. Your mother has to be a Jew. However, you can convert to Judaism. Prominent people have done that. It requires you to go through nine months of study and preparation of our religion and learning the holy books, the Torah and the Talmud."

"I am not ready to convert right now. I actually came to find out about the Spirit of Truth," replied Sebastian.

Moshe seemed a little perplexed. "What do you mean Spirit of Truth? We do believe that a messiah will come to save us. The Spirit of Truth is from the New Testament, the Bible. We as Jews do not believe in a Spirit of Truth."

"What about a messenger of the covenant?" Sebastian insisted. "I don't know of any messenger of the covenant. That is not mentioned in any of our holy books."

"But Malachi Chapter 3-1 talks about the messenger of the Covenant," said Sebastian pulling out his Bible and opening to the page he had marked. "I will send my messenger, who will prepare the way before me. Then suddenly the Lord you are seeking will come to his temple; the messenger of the covenant, whom you desire, will come," says the LORD Almighty.

The rabbi took one glance and quickly waved the Bible aside and said, "I know, I know, but that messenger is the Messiah, and he is yet to come." He continued, "You know there have been a lot of false messengers, and I urge you to be careful." He drew closer to Sebastian and whispered, "I presume you are Christian, and I don't wish to offend you, but your Jesus Christ, he was not the Messiah he claimed to be."

Sebastian was quite tempted to blurt out "so you are saying Jesus was a liar," but he controlled himself. Moshe was getting a bit irritated at this point it seemed.

"Have you heard of a mathematical code embedded in the structure of the Jewish scriptures?" asked Sebastian.

The rabbi replied, "I have but I would again be very careful of these studies. Some people claim that they took every fourth word in the Torah and it spelled out the word Yahweh."

"Seeing that you are interested in numbers, we do have the science of Kabbalah. There are many books that describe this. It is a mysterious science. Some say it is the soul of the Torah and contains the mystical meanings of the reason for our creation, the laws of the universe and the journey of the soul. Its proponents say it connects us to the Creator and helps find meaning in our lives."

"How do the numbers work?" enquired Sebastian politely. "Well," replied Rabbi Moshe Aaron, "I am not sure, and I know very little because I am pleased with reading the Torah and Talmud and rabbinical teachings of our great rabbis but it's something like this. Let me give you an example. If two words add up to the same value, they have the same spiritual meaning. So Elohim has the same meaning as nature, Ha Teva, which has the same meaning as a cup, Kos, because they each add up to eighty-six. Nature and Creator are one and the same. A cup is a desire to receive, so we can match nature by changing our desire to match."

Sebastian listened intently. Even though his patience was starting to wear thin, it would be disrespectful to cut the rabbi off. Finally he decided to change the topic.

"Getting back to the Messiah?" he injected politely.

"Yes, the Messiah," exclaimed the Rabbi. "Let's talk more about that. The Messiah would rebuild the sanctuary and gather the dispersed tribes of Israel. This has not happened, so he has not come. We will only know the Messiah after he has accomplished these things."

"I suppose that rules out Jesus, Muhammad and Buddha," Sebastian stated with a sense of unconvinced finality.

"Absolutely! That is why we don't believe in them," said the Rabbi.

"So what will the Messiah look like?" Sebastian asked.

"I really don't know and would not want to conjecture. Like I said, we will only know him after he has done what he is commissioned to do. Now, I really have to go." The rabbi wanted to end the conversation citing some personal chores.

Sebastian politely thanked the Rabbi and turned towards the door. He had hoped to get some clues at least from the oldest biblical religion, the first of the monotheistic three. He had just reached the top of the stairs outside in the compound and was about to make his way down when he felt a tap on his left shoulder and a hoarse voice saying, "Young man, do you have a minute?"

Surprised, Sebastian turned around suddenly to see an old, bent man looking at him straight in the eyes. He had apparently followed Sebastian outside.

In a heavy Hebrew accent he said in broken English, "I have been keeping these floors clean for thirty years to please the Almighty and have heard many stories. I heard you talking to Rabbi Moshe Aaron about a mathematical code. Have you heard of Frank Talmage? He was a luminary and with Joseph Dan he wrote a book *Studies in Jewish Mysticism* where he talks about how the Torah was structured on a mathematical pattern."

"Where can I get it?" Sebastian asked.

"I found it so inspiring that I bought many copies." Suddenly he pulled out a copy from under his cloak. "I got this for you."

Sebastian was taken aback. Was this a coincidence or was it destined to happen?.

As he thanked the old man and parted he heard these words from behind, "I know you are on a mission to find the truth. May the Almighty bless you."

CHAPTER THIRTEEN

THE TAXI HAD JUST DROPPED SEBASTIAN ON THE Via della Conciliazione, the main thoroughfare to St. Peter's Square, the huge courtyard adjoining the massive St. Peter's Basilica, one of the largest churches in the world. As he headed towards the impressive domed structure, Castel Sant'Angelo loomed to his right. The imposing cylindrical structure, once the tallest building in all of Rome, was built as the Mausoleum of Hadrian, the fourteenth Roman Emperor who ruled between 117 AD and 138 AD. Atop the castel stands a statue of the archangel Michael. Legend has it that Pope Gregory the great, patron saint of school children, had a vision that the angel Michael appeared here waving his sword to signal the end of the plague in 590 AD, giving the castle its name Castle of the Holy Angel. On the right lay the River Tiber, east of St. Peter's Basilica, the second longest river in Italy, which ran through the city of Rome. Occasionally Sebastian could see a tour boat cruising by with tourists taking pictures of the majestic basilica. Sebastian, walking at a brisk pace was already in St. Peter's Square with its circular courtyard, surrounded by columns. He paused in the middle near the obelisk for a minute and looked around. Sebastian wondered at the colossal Tuscan colonnades, four columns deep that covered the sides of the elliptical courtyard. Above the roof that was supported by these columns, several statues of popes, angels, St. Peter and even Jesus were erected like silent sentinels guarding one of the most revered churches of Christendom.

Without realizing Sebastian stepped on a round tile and looked around at the columns. The colonnades appeared only one row deep as if there were single column side by side. Three other columns behind each colonnade were not visible. This was one of the many optical illusions designed by Bernini.

The Egyptian obelisk, a long needle-like structure made of red granite towering forty-one metres into the sky was right before him. Straight ahead lay the monument built on the tomb of St. Peter, the fabulous St. Peter's Basilica with its famed, imposing dome planned by the great architect and painter Michelangelo. From the obelisk, Sebastian was able to see both fountains, the one designed in 1613 AD by Carlo Maderno on the right and the one created by Carlo Fontana in 1677 AD to the left.

Interestingly enough, the obelisk was a symbol of great power. There were similar obelisks in Washington and London, the military and financial capitals of the world. Here, in the middle of Rome, the obelisk symbolized religious dominance of a vast church with a billion followers and the control it exercised within the corridors of power.

The Congregation for the Doctrine of Faith is located in the Palace of the Holy Office in Rome. This is one of two extraterritorial properties owned by the Vatican outside Vatican City. Sebastian was supposed to meet with the assistant to the Prefect of the Congregation, the highest authority in the Congregation for the Doctrine of Faith. He had called them before he left Los Angeles, and had spoken to Cardinal Lorenzo Antonelli, who seemed very interested that a researcher from the United States wanted to learn more about the second coming of Christ from a Catholic perspective. But at the last minute Cardinal Antonelli had emailed Sebastian that he could not make it and instead he would send Monsignor Angelo Augustoni to meet him at a new venue, The Palazzo Del Governatorato in the Vatican Gardens, where the offices of the central administration for the Vatican are housed.

The Vatican Gardens cover more than half of the forty-four hectares of Vatican City. They are laden with gardens and fountains, and contain statues, a railway station and a communications tower for Radio Vatican, founded in 1931 AD by the Italian inventor and radio pioneer Guglielmo Marconi. Tours of the Vatican Gardens begin at the west entrance near the Vatican Museum but Sebastian was instructed to enter the Vatican Gardens through a special route, to the east of the Basilica near the Castle Santa Maria and then head towards the Palazzo Del Governatorato.

He passed by Piazza Santa Maria, a large courtyard with a fountain and two oak trees perfectly clipped to look like little domes. As Sebastian headed up the cobbled stairway towards the Palazzo Del Governatorato, he could see the papal court of arms of Benedict XVI on the lawn in front of the building. As he approached towards the main entrance, a silhouette of a figure clad in a white robe emerged, waving from the balcony on the first floor and shouted, "I will meet you at the main entrance."

Monsignor Angelo Augustino was a tall, bespectacled man in his early sixties with a comforting grin on his face.

After giving Sebastian a firm handshake he said, "Follow me," as he turned around and led him to a private study about thirty feet away. "Can I offer you some tea and biscuits," he said, and just as

Sebastian was about to answer, the monsignor was already pouring tea from a freshly brewed pot on the side table. Before Sebastian realized it, he was sitting on a luxurious brown leather chair facing the monsignor and sipping a fine blend of Earl Grey English tea.

"I was brought up Catholic," said Sebastian figuring it would be a good way to introduce himself and put the monsignor at ease by finding common ground.

"Wonderful, so you know the basics. I don't need to go over them then," replied Angelo Augustino.

"Actually that was a long time ago. Perhaps a short refresher might help."

Monsignor Augustino continued, "As you know we are the oldest church in the world and have a very systematic way of doing things. Our doctrines are clearly laid out, and I will be very glad to outline the fundamentals, but I suspect you already know something about the Catholic Church and its teachings from your upbringing. Let me tell you this, however, we have official interpretations of the Bible for the sake of unity and consistency. We do not encourage the faithful to come up with their own interpretations."

Sebastian nodded, "I know, and that is good. If everyone came up with their own, different understanding, there would be chaos."

Monsignor Augustino seemed pleased. Sebastian was a good listener and he already understood a valid point that had troubled so many that the monsignor had talked to before.

He continued, "The foundation of our faith is our Lord Jesus Christ, who is the saviour and part of the Trinity - Father, Son and Holy Ghost. And then there is Mother Mary and the saints. The saints have a special place and the ability to do miracles. A lot of the faithful have had their prayers answered and been healed by reaching out to the saints."

Sebastian knew that if he got into the details of Christianity and the Catholic faith it would turn into a never ending discussion. He had figured out at an early age that all religions claimed to be right, and the focus was taken away from the Creator in whom they all believed. Now the monsignor was talking about people praying to saints instead of God. So he got straight to the point.

"I am trying to find out about the Messenger of the Covenant?"

Monsignor Augustino recoiled, as if taken by complete surprise by the young man sitting across from him.

"I am sorry, but exactly who are you trying to find out about? You must be referring to the second coming of Christ, correct?"

Sebastian responded in a very polite and respectful tone, knowing that there was a bit of tenseness to the situation at hand.

"You know in the Bible, Jesus says in John 14:16, 'I shall ask the Father, and he will give you another Paraclete to be with you forever, the Spirit of truth,' and we know the Spirit of Truth will guide us to all truth and announce the things to come."

"Oh you mean the Spirit of Truth. That was Jesus."

"But does the Bible not say, 'I will ask the father and HE will send *another*'..." Sebastian's voice trailed off.

Monsignor Augustino quickly retracted. "I'm sorry, with all these terms, and asking about the Messenger of the Covenant, I forgot. The Spirit of Truth is the Holy Ghost."

"But 2000 years have gone by, and we don't have all the answers. The ordination of women, the integration of gays, abortion, divorce, and celibacy of the priests - these are all issues that have caused much division and pose a challenge to the Church. So I wanted to find out more about this from the Catholic perspective," Sebastian insisted. "And what about the Messenger of the Covenant mentioned in Malachi?"

Sebastian quickly pulled up the relevant quote from the Bible that was stored as a bookmark on his smart phone. "Behold, I am going to send My messenger, and he will clear the way before Me. And the Lord, whom you seek, will suddenly come to His temple; and the messenger of the covenant . . ."

He stopped as he noticed the monsignor fidgeting nervously as he cleared his throat.

Angelino clearly was not happy with the way this was turning out. This young lad was giving him a lecture on what problems the church was grappling with, and Sebastian realized he was treading on thin ice. Sebastian was tempted to bring out the issue of priests molesting boys but knew better.

"I am confused and need your help, but could it possibly be that the Messenger of the Covenant and the Spirit of Truth are the same?"

"Absolutely not," retorted Monsignor Augustino trying to hide his anger. "This is something from the Old Testament that the Jews believe in as a messiah, but we already know that Jesus Christ was the Messiah. Off the record, you and I both know that the Jews killed Jesus because they are waiting for another messiah, and they rejected the true Messiah. But the death and resurrection of Jesus was part of God's plan to save humanity because he took on our sins with his suffering. I am sorry but I cannot help you any more with this. All I can say is we have all we need, the Bible, the miracles, salvation and a great leader in the pope to overcome any challenges that might lie ahead. We don't need anything else."

Monsignor Augustino, now seemingly arrogant, decided to impress on Sebastian further.

"I don't know if you are aware, but our Lord Jesus Christ told Peter that he is the rock upon which his church would be built. This is the rock and we are the Catholic Church."

"But if there is something else you would like to enquire about I will be most pleased to shed some light on," he added, realizing that it was not befitting his character to lose his cool and be so curt as to sound rude or arrogant.

"There is nothing more," Sebastian replied politely.

He knew his time was up and any further questions would only cause an outburst of negative reaction on the part of the monsignor. So he thanked him for his valuable time and told him he would rethink in light of what information he had received from him. Apparently this seemed to satisfy Monsignor Augustino enough that he smiled back and said, "You are welcome. May the Lord be with you."

CHAPTER FOURTEEN

CAIRO IN JUNE IS DIRTY AND HOT. A BUSTLING CITY of more than seventeen million, it is the largest metropolis in the Middle East, and surpassed only by Lagos in Africa. As he rode by taxi towards one of the oldest universities in the world, the Al-Azhar University, the thoughts of scenes from the Ten Commandments, the epic movie he had watched as a kid, came to mind. This was the land of the mighty Pharoahs, the pyramids and the longest river in the world, the Nile.

Al-Azhar University is one of the oldest educational institutions in the world. Built during the period 971-988 AD, it is part of the famed Al-Azhar mosque, named after the prophet Muhammad's daughter Fatima. As the taxi sped along Port Said Street and turned left onto Al-Azhar Street, Sebastian got a glimpse of the three large minarets ahead, and what caught his eye was that one of the minarets had twin spires.

The cab driver let him off at the fifteenth century Barber's Gate. Sebastian entered into a large white marble courtyard built in the tenth century, towered by the three stately minarets. The courtyard, constructed during the Fatimid period is accented by rosettes and keel-arched panels over its white facade. This courtyard was originally the place students sat around a teacher and learned Arabic, Koran interpretations, and history through rote memorization - something that is still done today.

Adjacent to this was a large covered prayer hall and two religious schools called madrassas. Sebastian had not managed to get an appointment with a notable religious authority beforehand, and had taken his chances of just dropping by, knowing the zeal with which Muslim students would try and convert him. Students were scattered in groups of four or five throughout the courtyard and Sebastian presumed they were between classes. As he approached one group after another he realized that they hardly spoke English but stared at him intently. He felt out of place and hesitated, thinking he was treading on ground that he was not allowed. It was puzzling because he was not in the covered prayer hall. He also did not know how to start the conversation with them. Little did he realize that one or two students had slipped away into a tiny door on the far side. Suddenly a cloaked cleric, wearing a white turban started walking towards him. As he came closer he had a big grin and open arms and spoke in fluent English. "Salaam, peace. Are you looking for someone? How can I help you?"

Sebastian was taken by surprise but also relieved that he finally connected with someone, and was extended a form of hospitality. He did not want to shock this man by being too direct and by asking about someone coming after Muhammad, knowing how sensitive Muslims are to their prophet.

"I am here to ask some questions, to know more about Islam."
"Of course, of course. My name is Sheikh Muhammed el Nasr, and I will be most happy to help you understand our religion. You know it is one of the three major monotheistic religions and shares a lot of

commonality with Jews and Christians. But you come with me and we will talk, and I will explain to you about our great religion and our blessed prophet, Muhammad, peace be upon him. Come."

He beckoned Sebastian encouragingly in the direction of the small door from which he had emerged.

Sheikh Nasr led Sebastian across the courtyard into a small austere room with a small wooden table and two chairs. Except for a floor to ceiling bookshelf and window there wasn't much else.

"This is my time away from work, when I am not teaching. I like to look out into the courtyard towards the prayer hall and see the students meet each other and socialize and talk about Islam. There are scholars who look like and walk amongst the students. This provides students with a valuable learning experience without feeling intimidated. I have another office in the department of theology about two blocks away. You know this university is scattered over many buildings in this area, but my heart is still with this beautiful mosque and its architecture."

As Sebastian looked outside the window he could see a beautiful minaret.

"There are five minarets belonging to the mosque. The three tall minarets you see when you approach from the Barber's Gate entrance were built in the twelfth, thirteenth and fourteenth century by different kings."

When he returned to sit on one of the chairs, Sebastian noticed there were two cups of tea on the table.

"Turkish chai," said the Sheikh as he sat down on the other chair. "Let me tell you about Islam."

Sebastian knew he had to listen patiently. He had assumed the role of a student and authority here was absolute. The Sheikh began in an authoritative tone, as if he were addressing a student who knew very little.

"We believe that there is only one God, Allah and Muhammad, peace be upon him, was Allah's final prophet and messenger to mankind. Additionally there are four other pillars of Islam, and we have to do prayers, charity, fasting and the Hajj pilgrimage to Mecca. Islam is a way of life, it is a religion of peace. We as Muslims all accept that the Holy Koran is the final word of Allah, as revealed to our prophet and we also follow the teachings of our prophet, the Hadith and Sunnah."

Sebastian was so glad that the Sheikh was not going into details but just summarizing.

"There are two major sects in Islam, the Sunni and the Shia. The Shia sect split from mainstream Islam because they venerate the family of the Prophet Muhammad, may Allah shower peace and blessings upon him." To Sebastian's utter surprise the Sheikh stopped and looked at him as if to ask, "What else do you want to know?"

Sebastian read the cue perfectly. "Yes, I am interested in knowing about two things. First, is there a mathematical structure to the Koran, and second, if Muslims believe that some messiah will come before the end of time."

"Let me address the two questions," the Sheikh replied, in a typical instructor fashion.

Sebastian thought, *At least this guy's English is good, and he knows how to explain himself well.*

"The Koran sets the literary standard for excellence in Arabic and also has what we call memory bells. These memory bells stress certain syllables that allow us to know certain words in the following verse. This makes the Koran easy to memorize, and there are many millions around the world who know the Koran by heart. That would not be possible with a regular book spanning over five hundred pages."

"Wow," replied Sebastian, earnestly. "I did not know that." "And before I forget, there was an Egyptian biochemist living in America who claimed to have found a mathematical code in the Koran, but he rejected the Hadith and Sunna of our prophet, and tried to say that two verses in the Koran did not belong there because they were satanic. The Ulema declared him an infidel. This was many years ago, and the Ayatollah Khomeini put a death fatwa on him."

"You must be talking about Salman Rushdie. He is the one who wrote the Satanic verses," Sebastian said, hiding his excitement.

"No, no, it was someone else, an Egyptian living in America."

Sebastian tried to conceal his surprise, for this was very new to him. But before he had time to think and formulate a question, Sheikh Muhammad El Nasr continued.

"The hadith does have it that a Mahdi will come before the Day of Judgement. He will descend on Damascus. Jesus will also be there, and Jesus will pray behind the Mahdi." This was now sounding like a fascinating fairy tale to Sebastian and he tried to hide his amusement. "The Shia believe it is the return of their twelfth Imam Muhammad, son of Hasan Al-Askari who disappeared as a child of twelve some ten centuries ago and is hiding in a tunnel somewhere."

Sebastian let out a big smile.

"You think that is funny," Muhammad El Nasr said, his voice sounding a bit irritated.

"No, I just love your accent and the passion that you have when talking about Islam."

The Sheikh frowned as if he did not understand Sebastian's comment but continued, "Anyway, most Muslims believe that the holy Prophet Muhammad, may peace be upon him, is the final messenger and prophet but that Jesus will also return before the end of the world."

"But would that not make Jesus the last prophet," Sebastian asked, knowing this was going to be an unpleasant turn to the conversation since all Muslims firmly believed Muhammad was the final prophet.

"No, not at all. The Holy Prophet was the last in the line of prophets, but Jesus is an existing prophet before him, who will return to convince Christians to follow Islam."

Sebastian kept quiet. He could see the contradiction but the Sheikh could not. Or if the Sheikh realized it, he was doing a great job of keeping it to himself.

"So you don't believe in the messenger of the covenant, like the Christians?"

"You mean the Spirit of Truth mentioned in the Bible?" retorted the Sheikh.

"No the messenger of the covenant mentioned in Malachi 3." Sebastian wished he had a Bible on him but knew the risks of carrying it into a mosque in a Muslim country. "See even the Koran says in Surah 3 verse 81 that a messenger will come after the prophets," Sebastian recounted from his prepared notes.

"Never heard of it but when you quote the Koran I must refer to it to check your accuracy," said the Sheikh getting up and pulling a copy of the Koran from the shelf. "This is the translation by Marmaduke Muhammad Pickthall, who converted to Islam and was commissioned by the Nizam of Hyderabad, the richest person on the planet at that time."

The Sheikh read aloud from Pickthall's translation. *"And [recall, O People of the Scripture], when Allah took the covenant of the prophets, [saying], "Whatever I give you of the Scripture and wisdom and then there comes to you a messenger confirming what is with you, you [must] believe in him and support him." [Allah] said, "Have you acknowledged and taken upon that My commitment?" They said, "We have acknowledged it." He said, "Then bear witness, and I am with you among the witnesses."* (Koran 3:81)

"So this was our holy prophet Muhammad, peace be upon him," the Sheikh said confidently.

He was relieved that his beliefs were confirmed, but then he had been studying the Koran all his life in the original language, Arabic.

"Wait a minute. It says that the messenger will come after the covenant of the prophets, and since Muslims believe Muhammad was the final prophet, it must be someone after that. And it could not be Jesus either because he was also one of the prophets that made the covenant," prodded Sebastian.

The Sheikh was visibly upset now.

"No, the prophets all made the covenant with our prophet. He was the last messenger, so another messenger cannot come after him."

Sebastian was well prepared for this.

"But where does it say in the Koran that Muhammad was the final messenger?" El Nasr recoiled as if he had seen a snake. He never expected that. He figured, this young man does not know anything. After all, he is a foreigner, a non-believer. Within about fifteen seconds the Sheikh felt he had cooled down sufficiently so he spoke slowly and deliberately.

"Of course he was the final messenger. There has been no messenger after him. We don't need another messenger because our prophet brought the noble Koran, the final scripture from Allah, which has been perfectly preserved by divine decree. Whatever made you think he was not the final messenger? Every Muslim knows that. It is the fundamental article of faith that there is no God but Allah, and Muhammad, peace be on him, is the final messenger of Allah."

Sebastian suddenly decided to be scholarly, against his instincts. He knew he should behave very cautiously and respectfully. After all this was a Muslim country and the penalty for prophesying different beliefs, especially contradictory beliefs was severe. However, he had heard enough, and he knew the Sheikh was not speaking from the Koran but from his personal bias. The Sheikh had to be told that his scripture did not say what he was saying.

"Well, first, when you say 'and Muhammad is His messenger', Muhammad is dead and gone. A dead person cannot be a messenger. Muslims don't say Moses and Jesus are messengers, but that they *were* messengers. Muhammad was a messenger would be the correct way to say it, and," continued Sebastian without giving the Sheikh a chance to interrupt, "the verse in Chapter 33 verse 40 says 'He (Muhammad) was a messenger of God and the final prophet.' It does not say final prophet and messenger, or final messenger and prophet, or final messenger. The way it is worded means that prophet is not the same as a messenger."

"Muhammad, peace be upon him, was the final messenger, and he brought the final scripture, the Koran," the Sheikh said defiantly, hoping this further attempt would convince his guest. "All the messengers are prophets."

"But all the verses about prophets say they received the scripture and wisdom, and that messengers confirm existing scripture. So all prophets are messengers, but not all messengers are prophets. Let me show you." Sebastian asked for the translation the Sheikh was holding.

"I am sorry, I cannot give it to a non-Muslim. Only the pure can touch it."

Sebastian was on the verge of losing his temper and tried very hard to stay calm. He quickly browsed an online version of the Koran on his smart phone and showed the Sheikh a couple of selected verses.

> [3:79] Never would a human being whom GOD blessed with the scripture and prophethood say to the people, "Idolize me beside GOD." Instead, (he would say), "Devote yourselves absolutely to your Lord alone," according to the scripture you preach and the teachings you learn.

> [6:89] Those were the ones to whom we have given the scripture, wisdom, and prophethood. If these people disbelieve, we will substitute others in their place, and the new people will not be disbelievers.

"See, it fits in perfectly with Surah 3 verse 81 that all messengers are not prophets," continued Sebastian unabated. Then as if adding insult to injury he commented, "Messengers confirm and preach existing scriptures. Since God would not expect a prophet to keep the scripture for himself but preach it, all prophets are messengers but not all messengers prophets. This way 33:40 also makes perfect sense."

Sheikh Muhammad El Nasr was speechless. This unbeliever, this foreigner who knew nothing was giving him a lecture about the Koran. He knew the Koran and the vast library of Hadith backwards. As it is, he was already fuming and trying very hard to control his temper. Suddenly his tone changed.

"You do not know what you are talking about. You come here and pretend you want to learn, and then you say all these blasphemies about our revered prophet. Who taught you all this? Is this some Jewish plot to corrupt our religion? I think you had better leave because if other people find out what you are saying, you will get in very big trouble. Please go. And go quickly." With a wave of his hand, he beckoned Sebastian to leave immediately.

Before Sebastian could digest this response two guards appeared at the door out of the blue and escorted him through the courtyard and out of Barber's Gate, with a curious group of students peering at the saga that had just unfolded.

Before long Sebastian was back at the hotel. It was late evening and next morning was his flight back to Los Angeles. He had a couple of hours to reflect back on the day's events before he retired for the night.

CHAPTER FIFTEEN

THAT NIGHT WHILE READING THROUGH SOME OF his refer- ence books, Sebastian made an important discovery. After his interview with Jim Stone he had picked up a copy of the novel *Contact* by Carl Sagan. He remembered that there was a movie by the same name about a lady astronaut, played by the accom- plished actress Jodie Foster, who ventures into outer space and listens to these coded messages coming from deep out there. So he had decided to pickup the novel just out of curiosity. Towards the end of the novel, about three and a half hours later, Sebastian, who was occasionally dozing off but could not put down the novel, saw the following on page 433: "My fondest hope for this book is that it will be made obsolete by the pace of real scientific discovery." This phrase jolted him and he put the novel down and sat up from a lying position. *Is Carl Sagan saying that we could actually receive a mathematically coded message from outer space? Or have we already received such a message, and Carl Sagan is alluding to it. Is this fact or fiction? Does he know something that we do not? And what about the Sheikh's reference to some Egyptian biochemist removing two verses from the Koran?* The *Satanic Verses*, by Salman Rushdie was published in 1986, and Carl Sagan wrote

Contact the same year. While Carl Sagan received accolades for his book, Salman Rushdie, winner of the Booker prize, was subsequently condemned by a fatwa and went into hiding. Things seemed to come together. Perhaps there was a person around, possibly of Egyptian origin, who had found a mathematical code, which resulted in two verses being chucked out of the Koran and both Carl Sagan and Salman Rushdie capitalized on this and came up with novels! Maybe it was this person who sent him the script, and maybe it was this person who also went underground.

Sebastian flew into Los Angeles in the midst of ominous clouds on the horizon. He wondered what lay ahead.

No one was home when Sebastian entered his apartment. He had called out to Gracie but there was no response. The bedroom was empty. In the kitchen there was an envelope on the counter that Sebastian opened. A folded note in the envelope read, "I am at Julie's. Have left an interesting clip for you to read. I found this newspaper clip, maybe it will help with all that math stuff and religion you are researching. Sorry, but it is old and ripped on one side and most of the article is missing. Call me when you get back." Aunt Julie was Gracie's only surviving sibling and lived in San Diego. Gracie had gone to the local library and searched the archives and the internet and found something she felt was relevant to her young nephew's research.

Sebastian looked at the clipping. All it said was 'Tucsonan says Computer proves the ...' The rest was cut off. Even the name of the journalist below was blacked out. Sebastian studied the clip. He figured based on the font size and width that there were five letters missing at the end of the heading. The words Bible, Torah and Koran, sacred scriptures of Christians, Jews and Muslims all had five alphabets. It could be anyone of these books or something else. This was not telling him much. It was interesting that the journalist's name was blacked out, and there was no way to tell which newspaper this was from or the date of publication. He wondered, *Maybe if this was true, it created much controversy and the journalist wanted to go into hiding.* Something had happened. Something that was not good. A feeling inside his bones told him this might have to do with the script he had received. He decided he simply had to go to Tucson. The script seemed to be written by an educated, intellectual person who might possibly have been a professor at the University of Arizona.

His four weeks were up, and he knew Jim Stone would not be at all happy with this delay. He shot off an email to Jim that he would see him in three days, and that he had to go to Tucson because something very interesting had turned up. Sebastian prayed hard that he would find the answers in Tucson; otherwise he had nothing to go back to Jim with. He might very well lose his job. It was a do or die situation. The trip to Italy and the Middle East had not gotten him very far. Thank God he had one more lead, courtesy of Gracie.

Sebastian unpacked and decided to retire for the evening. He would book his ticket to Tucson tomorrow. As he emptied his bags he noticed the book given to him by the old man sweeping the interior floors at the Hurva. He picked it up, walked over to the living room and stretched himself horizontally on the sofa with his head propped up on one side. Then he immersed himself in reading the book.

To his surprise, *Studies in Jewish Mysticism* was filled with interesting facts about Kabbalah and numbers and their spiritual meaning. Then came the shocker. On page 82 he read:

> *The people [Jews] in France made it a custom to add [in the morning prayer] the words: "Ashrei temimei derekh [blessed are those who walk the righteous way]," and our*

> *Rabbi, the Pious, of blessed memory, wrote that they were completely and utterly wrong. It is all gross falsehood, because there are only nineteen times that the Holy Name is mentioned [in that portion of the morning prayer]... and similarly you find the word 'Elohim nineteen times in the pericope of Ve-'elleh shemot. Similarly, you find that Israel were called "sons" nineteen times, and there are many other examples. All these sets of nineteen are intricately intertwined, and they contain many secrets and esoteric meanings, which are contained in more than eight large volumes. Furthermore, in this section there are 152 (19x8) words.*

Sebastian suddenly sat up, then stood and started pacing the living room.

He thought, *Omigod, so there is a mathematical code that existed in the Jewish scriptures and it is based on the same number as mentioned in the script!*

However, the information in the script was not to be found in any of the scriptures of the three major monotheistic religions, at least not directly. Could it be that it was taken from more than one scripture, possibly from all three scriptures? And why nineteen?

It completely took him by shock that the very synagogue he had chosen to visit in Jerusalem, the Hurva, was actually built upon ruins by followers of Rabbi Judah, the very person mentioned in the book he had picked up at the Hurva, a book given to him by an old man sweeping the floors! Rabbi Judah was the very person who had found a mathematical code in the Jewish scriptures. Maybe it was part of destiny that Sebastian went there.

The number nineteen is not an easy number to work with, thought Sebastian. *Moreover it is a prime number, and when we take the two numbers ten and nine that add to nineteen, not only do the sum of the first powers add to nineteen, the difference of the second powers, one hundred less eighty-one, equal nineteen as well.*

He quickly double-checked the numbers.

$10^1 + 9^1 = 19$

$10^2 - 9^2 = 100 - 81 = 19$

One and nine were also the first and last numbers of the counting system and in that sense symbolized the Alpha and Omega, qualities of God. It seemed to him to be a good choice. Furthermore, it was an interesting number as well. Centuries ago, before the invention of numbers, a system of Gematrical Values was developed where alphabets were given values. In the Roman numeral system, X was 10, C was 50 and L was 100. Similarly for Aramaic and Arabic, the word that means one is Wahid, and it has four letters. These 4 letters occupy positions six, one, eight and four in the list of alphabets in both these languages and the sum of these numbers is nineteen.

Sebastian wrote down the first eight letters of the alphabet in both Aramaic and Hebrew from the Gematrical Value table, In Aramaic, alaph=1, beth=2, gamal=3, dalat=4, heh=5, waw=6, zain=7, heth=8.

In Arabic, alif=1, ba=2, jeem=3, daal=4, ha=5, waw=6, za=7, ha=8.

Then he calculated the Gematrical Value from both tables for Wahid waw alaph heth dalat - 6 1 8 4 = 19

wow alef ha daal - 6 1 8 4 = 19

Wasn't the greatest quality of God, according to the scriptures that HE was One and there was none like HIM?

"Hear O Israel, the Lord your God is One" (Deuteronomy 6:4).

So nineteen symbolized that God is One.

There were so many other things that came to his mind, based on his knowledge of astronomy and medicine taught to him by his parents. Haley's comet comes around every seventy-six years. A full term fetus has a term of two hundred and sixty-six days after fertilization. The earth, moon and sun align in the same plane every nineteen years. There were five hundred and seventy years between the birth of Jesus and Muhammed, founders of the world's two largest religions. All these were multiples of nineteen. *Maybe the number nineteen is the Creator's signature on his creation!* Sebastian thought.

He reflected on the date of the moon landing, a historic event for the human race. It was on July 20, 1969. Sebastian wrote the numbers next to each other 7 20 1969.

He took out his calculator and divided the number 7201969. It was divisible by nineteen

A thought struck him. In Europe they put the day first. So he reversed the month and day and entered 20 7 1969. Again it was a multiple of nineteen. This was no coincidence.

There was one more thing left for Sebastian to do. The Script was not very long. He sat down at his laptop and typed it into Microsoft Word. More than three hours later, when finished, he got the program to count the words. There were exactly six thousand three hundred and forty six words.

"Omigosh," he claimed excitedly and aloud, "this is not only divisible by nineteen but the numbers six, three, four and six also add up to nineteen!"

He wondered what the probability would be of a number being divisible by 19 and having its digits also add up to 19. *Pretty small, I would say,"* he thought

Brimming with excitement, Sebastian lay awake the whole night.

CHAPTER SIXTEEN

TUCSON IS SITUATED IN PIMA COUNTY ARIZONA, sixty-eight miles north of the Mexican border. The desert to the north is filled with cactus plants and the winter can bring frost. In summer, the daytime temperature can hit one hundred and ten degrees Fahrenheit. As Sebastian stepped out onto the tarmac from the small American Eagle Embraer shuttle run by American Airlines, he was greeted by a very warm blast of hot air. It felt like an oven and he was glad he was wearing a baseball cap. Outside the terminal he flagged a cab to take him to the main library at the University of Arizona.

University of Arizona has a lot of students with a Middle Eastern background, who prefer climate similar to what they are accustomed to back home. The University itself is spread over several blocks and includes a stadium for the Arizona Wildcats football club. Bordered by Campbell and Euclid Avenues to its east and west, most of the university buildings are south of Speedway Boulevard, a major thoroughfare that runs east to west across the city. The setting of the university is quite beautiful, red tiled low-rise pink buildings against a backdrop of mountains to the north. The main library, where Sebastian was headed, is just across Fourth Street from the Arizona Stadium, home to the Wildcats.

One reason for Sebastian choosing the university was that it is home to the Arizona Center for Judaic Studies. The main library itself is frequented by people of Turkish, Egyptian and Israeli origin. As Sebastian browsed through a list of religious books, he noticed a certain title that caught his interest had been checked out and not returned. The title of the book was *The Computer Speaks: God's message to the world.*

Sebastian was very excited. He approached the librarian and enquired about this title and when it might be back.

"I don't know, it was checked out several years ago, before my time," answered the librarian.

Sebastian figured someone wanted to keep the book for themselves or did not want it to be available and had taken it out of circulation. He spent the next hour going through newspaper clippings hoping to find an intact copy of the one Gracie had given him but was not able to. While quite disappointed, he was at the same time grateful that he had stumbled upon this clue about the book. He was in the right city. Something had happened here. There was definitely a link to the newspaper clip that Gracie had left.

He browsed a bit more, this time in the religious section and then decided to leave and get some lunch. Coming out of the main library, he turned left and then headed north on Cherry Ave. towards University Boulevard on his way west towards Euclid Avenue. As he walked on The Eastern Mall, below him lay the 118,000 square foot Pacheco Integrated Learning Center for freshmen. Dedicated in honour of the nineteenth president of the university, Manuel Pacheco, this facility provided freshmen access to core classes, advisors and a round the clock computer lab.

Several eateries are lined along university boulevard ranging from fast food Chinese Panda Express to traditional American Johnny Rockets. Sebastian decided on some Mexican food and chose Chipotle's over La Salsa. He grabbed a chicken burrito and headed west to Euclid. He wished he could find some ice cream, perhaps a Ben and Jerry's or Baskin Robbins but nothing showed up. Turning left towards Sixth street he wondered what more he could do. Yes, he had found strong indication that there was something related that had happened here, but it seemed a dead end. There were no more clues, no more leads to pursue. A lot of time was simply wasted, and he had to go back to Jim empty-handed without the smoking gun Jim had demanded, hoping Jim would still let him keep his job. It seemed such a shame. After all, the script he had picked off the dust pile back at Pinnacle seemed so genuine and so powerful. It had answers that could change the world for the better, and remove a lot of the chaos that existed on the planet.

"So sad I got nowhere," he muttered, as he approached the intersection of Euclid and Sixth street. "At least it answered many of my questions."

There was a bus stop on the other side of the street and so he decided to head back to the Hampton Inn on South Tucson Blvd and then return to Los Angeles the next day.

Sebastian patiently waited for the bus in the hot summer weather. With the temperature well past a hundred degrees Fahrenheit, he was sweating profusely. Even with a hat, he could feel perspiration running down his forehead and cheeks. Then he saw it. At first he had hardly noticed the small white single-storey stucco building diagonally across the street on the north-west corner. It seemed dilapidated and lifeless, with no cars in the parking lot or any lights on inside, but there was a sign on the wall he could hardly read because it was discoloured and covered mostly in mud. However, he could still make out the words 'Happiness is' and 'God' and it aroused his curiosity. The bus, it seemed, was not going to be there for a while because he could look a far distance down Sixth street, and it was nowhere in sight. He decided to check this building out.

He used a stone to dislodge some of the mud that had been lodged on the wall for what seemed was many years and unveiled most of the letters on the side of the wall to uncover the words "Happiness is devotion to God." It reminded him of the script. Did it not say that God was omnipotent and our happiness lay in meeting His purpose here on earth? Sebastian decided to see if he could go inside. He went around the corner to the front where three steps ascended onto a small patio leading to the front door. He tried to open it, but it was locked. A thought struck him and he decided to go to the side door. To his surprise it was unlocked.

Inside was a strange sight to behold. He had stepped into a kitchen that was very clean with a strong smell of disinfectant. It was bright, with sunshine streaming in through the window. The walls were yellow and the floor was covered in linoleum, popular during the seventies and eighties. The almond stove and fridge looked almost as if they were meticulously cleaned up after a mess. Looking through the kitchen door on the opposite side of the entrance, he could barely make out a large room engulfed in almost total darkness. But it was not empty, there seemed to be something inside. As he walked in, surrounded by an eerie silence, he realized that it was furniture, mostly chairs and they were in disarray, some turned over and some broken. There had obviously been a fight in here, and maybe it moved out to the kitchen. Perhaps even a crime scene. which was cleaned up afterwards. The building was clearly abandoned. *Interesting*, he thought. *There is something that I am just not figuring out.* The drapes had all been pulled across the windows and it seemed stuffy - and hot. Pangs of desperation again overcame him.

What was he trying to accomplish? What did he expect to find here? Trying to chase down what happened many years ago was not practical. Did he really expect to find the person who wrote the script alive and well somewhere in this city without something more to work with? For a moment he regretted even coming to this city and the freaking hot climate. Already he had missed the bus. He turned around, and suddenly the disappointment started setting in. His heart felt weighed down. Even though he knew he was not getting anywhere, this last bit of hope that he had when he wiped the mud off the wall had now melted away. He simply was not getting any breaks. *Luck is not on my side.* He turned around sadly to head back out.

But fate was not to abandon him. Just then he felt a slight breeze. It was almost refreshing. Tucson weather can change suddenly in summer just before an imminent thunderstorm. The wind outside was gusting, and it was enough to part a set of drapes that covered a slightly open window. A ray of bright sunshine beamed in and caught his attention. What really caught his eye, as he followed the beam down to the carpet, was a small piece of paper shining brightly in the sunshine as it flew in the wind. He darted across, between the upturned furniture, and picked it up fearing it might get blown around and lost.

He would have expected the paper to be quite dusty, but there was no dust on it, just like the script he had found in the dusty pile back at Pinnacle. It was reassuring and his hopes built up a little. Once back out in the sunlight, Sebastian looked at the slip of paper. The paper had fourteen numbers, arranged in two columns and seven rows. But what shocked him was what else was there. Written in cursive, it read, "We have given you seven pairs and the great . . ." The rest of the sentence was cut off. Again, there seemed to be about five letters missing.

We are back to the Torah, the Bible or the Koran. Or something else. Why did all the major religious scriptures have to consist of five letter names.

That was strange. It reminded him of the news clip Aunt Gracie had given him that read "Tucsonan says computer proves the --." Seemed like someone had gotten to both the newspaper clipping and to this note and removed the name of the source of the script that Sebastian needed so urgently. He would go back and see if he could turn the lights on and find the rest of that slip if it was still there. He was sure the hydro would have been cut off years ago, but he could use a flashlight. Then he retraced his steps to the side door and went outside hoping to go buy a flashlight. An idea struck him.

I could walk over to the window and pull the drapes apart to get some more light. As he turned around to open the side door again he found the door was locked shut. Somehow he had managed to lock it behind him when he had left. He was meant to go in only once, find the paper and then never be able to get back in. Destiny was in control. Once again, he felt that an unseen force was playing its hand.

When he got to the hotel it hit him like a ton of bricks. The script had seven little figures that looked like apples. Now he recollected that they looked like pears. Could that be an encoded sign that it was seven pairs and not seven pears? Seven pairs meant fourteen. There were seven pairs of numbers on the slip. He simply had to get those numbers analysed. This just might be the smoking gun he could present to Jim. He was really excited now.

This latest discovery invigorated him as he travelled back to the Hampton Inn. He decided to take a break. A twenty minute swim in the hotel pool followed by a sauna made him feel like a new man. He treated himself to a delicious sirloin steak dinner at Finnegan's near the hotel and retired for the night. The flight to Los Angeles was early in the morning.

CHAPTER SEVENTEEN

TED JACOBSEN HAD ARRIVED EARLY THAT MORNING to work at the University of Southern California. As assistant professor of mathematics he would usually get to work an hour before classes started to prepare for the morning class. Today he had to mark some quizzes. Over a cup of coffee he opened his email and saw a name that he had not heard from in several years but a name he instantly recognized. It was his buddy from high school, Sebastian Girard. They had had so many good times together, been on the same soccer team and debated against each other. Moreover, they complemented each other, Ted being very strong in the sciences and Sebastian with the arts. Almost inseparable for eight years, and then suddenly it was over. Both graduated high school and went their separate ways, he into the information technology field that he loved and Sebastian into film school.

Now Sebastian was writing to him and Ted seemed a bit surprised, although he welcomed the contact. He wondered what it could possibly be and quickly opened the email.

The email was not really what he expected. Besides the customary greeting there was a cryptic note.

"Really need your help. This might be big, very big. Please see these numbers below. There is something extraordinary about them. Can you please analyze and get back to me asap at 555-1838? Cannot tell you more now."

64 380
48 276
53 300*
44 324
16 150
31 200
36 225

Ted stared at the email for a minute. It sounded urgent as if Sebastian was in a desperate situation and pressed for time. It was not like him to write such curt messages especially without some kind of explanation. Ted really thought an email from an old friend, after such a long time, would contain more details, like how Sebastian was doing, where was he living and if he was married. But Ted loved working with numbers and solving riddles especially those 'magic cubes' where numbers were added along rows, columns or diagonals to come up with some pattern. He glanced at the numbers, seven rows of two numbers each, and at once started observing some patterns that were different from your usual Sudoku.

And what was the significance of the * in the third row?
Sounded kind of mysterious.

He knew Sebastian would not just send him a puzzle out of the blue to solve. And why was it so urgent? At once Ted made some observations. The numbers started with a square of eight, sixty-four and ended with a square of fifteen, two hundred and twenty-five. There were seven rows, and eight taken from fifteen left seven, which was the number of rows. There were also three more squares, sixteen, the square of four, thirty six, the square of six and three hundred and twenty four, the square of 18. What was also interesting was that the first number, and the last number, both squares added up to another square, 289, which was the square of 17. This was pretty interesting. He quickly added all the numbers and they came up to 2147. The sum of these digits, two, one, four and seven was fourteen and there were fourteen numbers in the email that added up to this number. Since 2147 was an odd number he quickly started dividing these by the prime numbers 3,5,7, 11, 13, 17 and so on and found that this number was only divisible by 19 and 113 - two prime numbers. *Very interesting*, he thought, *but that does not tell me anything else.*

Ted knew that primes were used widely in encryption algorithms. Two large primes multiplied together were practically impossible to break down into their factors, even with supercomputers. The large numbers were presented as the public key while the factors known only to the algorithm devisors would be the private key.

Quickly, he added all the digits of the above numbers and it came to 113. "Another prime. I am getting somewhere. This is the same number when we divide the total by nineteen."

Ted was getting late for his morning class, so he decided to take another look at the numbers later on.

Later that night he decided to start doing some calculations by adding columns. His focus was to see if there was a pattern, perhaps based on 19 or 113. None of the rows added up to a multiple of 19 or 113. Neither did any of the columns. But he did find something interesting in that the cumulative sum of all the numbers in the first three rows added up to 1121, or 19 times 59. Again, a multiple of two primes. This was where there was the *. It also meant the other 4 rows added up to the total 2147 minus 1121 or 1026, 19 x 54

He then decided to do the same thing with the second, third and fourth rows this time including the rows surrounding the row with the asterisk. Again, he came up with the same pattern. The three rows added up to 1045 or 19 times 55. Again, this meant that the other four rows not included, added up to 2147 minus 1045 or 1102, which is 19 x 58. Things were now really getting interesting.

Then Ted decided to do another series of calculations. Instead of adding the numbers in the rows, he added each digit that made up a number.

The result almost blew his socks off. He had never seen numbers like this in his life. Was this even possible? or was it a giant coincidence? There was no mathematical reason for this, it had to be by deliberate design. The fact that an asterisk was placed in the right position definitely pointed to this as no coincidence.

In each of the four calculations, he could take the sum of the digits, multiply by 19 and come up to the sum of the numbers! The sum of the digits of the first three rows came to 59, the digits of the following four rows added to 54. The sum of digits of rows surrounding and including the * added to 55 and the rest of the rows digits added to 58.

This was mind-boggling. It was like several dice that fell in a perfect order. Only we were dealing with 14 numbers each having a possibility from one to a thousand. That would be a thousand multiplied by itself 14 times, with each of these involving 112 digit and number sums calculations. He arrived at a very, very large number.

Ted quickly estimated how long it would take a supercomputer to work this out. The supercomputer he had access to could compute 43 trillion calculations per second. He multiplied this by the number of seconds in a year and divided it into the first number. The result would be the number of years it would take this computer to figure out all the possibilities and arrive at this set of numbers. The answer came to several hundred billion years, way more than the age of the universe. He had to get hold of Sebastian and let him know right away.

* * * *

Sebastian had been through a long night filled with anxiety. There were so many things on his mind. He was hoping Ted would find something. Then there was the meeting with Jim.

What would he say if Ted came up with nothing? Would he still have a job? Was this all a big mistake? It was a good thing that Gracie was not home yet, away visiting her sister because he was a wreck and he knew Gracie would not be able to bear to see him like this.

At first he thought it was the ringing of the alarm clock. Had he set it for the wrong time? It was 2 a.m. in the morning. Then he realized it was the phone. He prayed everything was okay with Gracie. With some trepidation he picked it up without even glancing at the call display to see who it was from.

The voice on the other end sounded excited. He could hardly make out what the person was saying or who it was. Then he realized it was Ted.

"I got something for you, but tell me first where in heaven's name did you get those numbers?"

"Why, did you find something?" Sebastian asked, doubting his own question.

Ted continued as if he had not even heard Sebastian, and he did not even wait for an answer to his own question.

"Those numbers are so powerful that they will blow your socks off."

Even though Sebastian had somehow wanted to hear that he asked a rhetorical question.

"What do you mean exactly? What can be so special about them?"

"Sebastian, those numbers could not have been generated by humans, even with the aid of super computers!" Ted replied emphatically, and then proceeded to explain all the details to Sebastian.

As he hung up the phone, after profusely thanking Ted and promising to keep in touch, he collapsed on the bed. He had not even realized he had been standing. This was a dream. After a few minutes his mind and body settled down and then his brain started working overtime.

"Omigosh, the numbers on the slip added to 2147, and those digits added to 14, or 7 x 2." This was a sign of the 7 pairs.

And, as he remembered from his reading of the King James Bible,

"I will raise them up a Prophet from among their brethren, like unto thee, and will put my words in his mouth; and he shall speak unto them all that I shall command him. And it shall come to pass, that whosoever will not hearken unto my words which *he shall speak in my name*, I will require it of him." [Deuteronomy 18:18]

This person will speak *In the Name of God* and this phrase also has fourteen letters, or seven pairs, and the seven little pears at the bottom of the script were telling him this! He had known from the time he read the script that the information was so heavy that it could not be from anybody else but the Creator Himself.

Sebastian's belief in what the script said was now turning to certainty. All those things that it contained were becoming stark reality.

CHAPTER EIGHTEEN

SEBASTIAN WALKED IN UNANNOUNCED INTO JIM stone's office. Having exceeded the time allotted to find a smoking gun by over two weeks, he did not want to give Jim the opportunity to grill him. He would have loved to have met the deadline Jim had set, but he could not walk in empty-handed.

Jim looked up, taken aback at the sudden appearance of Sebastian.

"Hi, can I come in?" Sebastian asked as he stepped into the office, and proceeded on seeing Jim's nod into the same over-stuffed brown leather chair he had sat in when he was interviewed for the job. To Sebastian's surprise, Jim was not upset at all. His next words put Sebastian at ease.

"I told you four weeks because I knew it would take at least eight. Tell me what did you find out?"

Sebastian filled Jim in on all the details, his trips to Rome and the Middle East and more details from the script, finally mentioning the findings of the last couple of days about the seven pairs. Jim listened very intently and then replied choosing his words carefully.

"I appreciate all the efforts you have made and expenses you incurred. There seem to be some very evident truths backed by compelling facts, but it has to be presented in a way that appeals to the viewing public."

"How should it be presented? We cannot put a spin on this, can we?" Sebastian asked.

"No. I was not suggesting that. As you know the content has strong religious overtones. We cannot make a movie projecting religion, especially something so controversial that claims that all religions are wrong," Jim replied.

Sebastian seemed to agree. "I know. But we are not pushing any religion as right or wrong. We would simply be making people aware of certain unified beliefs and answers to questions that they are yearning for."

Jim quickly retorted, "Sebastian, people cannot handle the truth." He continued, "But what we can do is present it as a fictional story. I know you can do it."

This turn of events made Sebastian squirm. He was glad that he still had the job and the confidence of Jim but it also seemed a bit too challenging. There was already quite a bit of effort required to turn the abstract and philosophical concepts and numerical facts he had uncovered into a movie script, but now Jim was telling him to write it as a fictional story.

"That is the only way we can move forward on this, young man. Go, you have a lot of work to do. Show me a draft in about three weeks."

Sebastian thanked Jim for the opportunity and excused himself.

* * * *

Sebastian had always believed in an almighty Creator. From high school science courses he learned of the intricacies of everything from atoms to galaxies held up by invisible pillars, the design of life giving water and its purification and circulation through evaporation and the balance in nature. He found it hard to believe when religion portrayed God as having been caught by surprise by the devil, and watching as a feeble bystander as His creation suffered. Some had even suggested that God wept for us because He loved us and yet His hands were tied and He was powerless to help. He even did not agree with giving a gender to the Creator. According to him, anyone who could create such a vast universe spanning billions of light years was too majestic to be imagined by our finite brains. We were these powerless, insignificant creatures in a universe of gigantic proportions. Only we thought too much of ourselves, were preoccupied with materialism, loved to argue and thought we could make our own destiny.

Once back in his office, Sebastian was dealing with some heavy material and putting a lot of thought into what he was going to write. The script that had started it all had now become a startling document with a strong connection to a mathematical proof, the Spirit of Truth and the Messenger of the Covenant. While his trip abroad had been met with a muted reaction by religious leaders of different faiths, his trip to the Hurva had paid off. The old man who had given him the book, *Studies in Jewish Mysticism* was certainly the highlight of that trip. He wondered why they were all covering up or steeped in ignorance about this coming Messiah. Human bias was such a destructive thing especially when people made up their minds on the wrong things. He was now determined more than ever to be as objective as he could in writing this true story as a fictional account.

It seemed to Sebastian that just about every novelist who wrote fiction tried to convince the reader that it was fact. He remembered the novel Da Vinci Code by Dan Brown. Here he was trying to do the opposite, trying to present fact but convince the readers it was fiction, hoping they would buy it. That would be quite a challenge.

Presenting the material was another challenge in itself. The advent of this mathematical code would mark the first physical evidence for the existence of a creator and presenting it to a mostly secular audience, with atheists and fanatical religionists on either side of the divide, and a lot of doubtful people in the middle, was complicated. Telling them the purpose of their life, and why there is chaos and misery seemingly ignored by a loving God, would be a handful. Telling them that God was in full control, and that allowing Satan to inflict bad things upon us was actually a mercy from Him to remind us to mend our ways was not going to be easy at all.

Sebastian had never believed that bad things came from a loving God. The script had opened his eyes to the fact that Satan was behind all things bad. According to the script, there was a Great Feud where the rebellious creatures were overpowered and sent down to Earth to prove their loyalty to God or Satan. He remembered references to this in the Scriptures he had read.

You, Lucifer, said in your heart: "I will scale the heavens. Above the stars of God. I will set up my throne. I will take my seat on the Mount of Congregation, in the recesses of the North. I will ascend above the tops of the clouds; I will be like the Most High!" [Isaiah 14:13-15]

Say, "Here is awesome news. That you are totally oblivious to.
I had no knowledge previously, about the feud in the High Society

I am inspired that my sole mission is to deliver the warnings to you.

Your Lord said to the angels, "I am creating a human being from clay.

Once I design him, and blow into him from My spirit, you shall fall prostrate before him.

The angels fell prostrate, all of them, except Satan; he refused, and was too arrogant, unappreciative." [Koran 38:67-74]

For a moment the pangs of depression again overtook him as he pondered the hopelessness of the task ahead. Yet on the bright side, telling people who were suffering that they could achieve perfect lives if they only followed God's law and passed the test, might inspire hope in them.

But Sebastian always cherished giving people hope. He remembered that after the death of his parents, it was only hope and perseverance that had brought him this far. Without hope all was lost. He had to continue. He had to write this fictional story.

Sebastian was told at a young age that according to the scriptures we were all here because Adam and Eve ate from the forbidden tree but this never sat quite right with him. Why would we be paying for the sins of others? Why *should* we be paying for the sins of others? This went against his belief of a fair God. On the other hand, the script gave an account of God having gathered all the souls before we came here and gave us the choice, and we all agreed to taking this test. The latter just made a lot more sense.

A new set of social etiquette, not as commandments to obey blindly but ones proven to be beneficial to mankind, would probably not be received well. Imagine a world with true democracy where the 51% majority does not force their opinions on a 49% minority.

What about making the murderer support the victim's family along with his own, so the state would not have to support both families, thereby eliminating the expensive and inhuman prison system at the same time? An economic system where everyone takes care of their own relatives by paying a percentage of income - it would be efficient, reduce burden on social services and taxpayers and there would be a lot fewer tax evaders. People could certainly buy into this. And yet he feared the human resistance and stubbornness to change would create a backlash.

Certainly the age of responsibility would be a matter of contention. Religious leaders ruled mostly by fear to keep the flock in line. Tales of an angry God willing to put people into a burning hell fire for their sins were abound. People could not fathom the notion that someone who died before a certain age could automatically go to heaven. *Even in this world, a court does not try someone too immature or unfit to stand trial.* Sebastian knew that people would question, "If someone is really, really bad and dies a day before they reach the age of responsibility, do you mean to say they will go to heaven?" He smiled. God is the one who signs the death certificate at the appointed time. If a person deserves hell, they simply will not die before that age. It seemed so simple to him - it was all a matter of accepting God's omniscience and omnipotence.

Sebastian collected his thoughts. He thought about the mathematical code and its relation to the number nineteen. He recounted that the digits 1 and 9 were the first and last numbers of our counting system, the Alpha and Omega. The Creator was referred to as the Alpha and Omega. Because the script emphasized monotheism and the oneness of the creator, Sebastian looked up the word 'one' in the Hebrew language. The four letters that made up the word one, were the sixth, first, eight and fourth letters of the alphabet. Those numbers added up to nineteen. In Arabic, the sister language to Hebrew, the word *Wahid* meaning one, also had four letters that had the same position in the alphabet and added to nineteen. This script was authorized by God - but the one who delivered it had probably been assassinated by those possessed with fanaticism and vested interests.

He recalled Carl Sagan's *Contact* written in 1986 about a mathematically coded document sent from outer space. In the same year, a Booker Prize winning author, Salman Rushdie had written *The Satanic Verses*. Could it be possible that there was a link between the two? Is it possible that the mathematical code had discovered two verses from a scripture that weren't supposed to be there, and the person who discovered this code was assassinated for suggesting this? Could that little white building in Tucson be the crime scene?

All the popular religions believed there would be a messiah coming to save humanity, but they could not agree on his identity. The Jews were still waiting for the Messiah. The Spirit of Truth, which Christians have been waiting for 2000 years, who would guide to all truth and announce things to come, had obviously not come because none of this had happened. Mankind was still left with many problems and even more pressing questions. How was he going to explain to them the true identity of this messenger of the covenant prophesized in Malachi by Jesus in the Bible and by Muhammed in the Koran. One of the things to come was the end of the world, but there were so many false predictions, so many tricksters and so much skepticism. It was impossible to give out this date without losing credibility and being deemed as a nutcase. To incorporate the seven pairs into this was even more daunting. According to the script not only were the seven pairs used to calculate the end of the world, the story of the seven sleepers of Ephesus who were resurrected after *three hundred years increased by nine* was also related to this. Three hundred solar years were equal to three hundred and nine lunar years.

According to the script, the world would end in 1710 AH or 2280 AD. Both these numbers were divisible by 19. These two dates represented calendars used by the world's two major religions, Christianity and Islam. Sebastian subtracted 1710 from 2280 and came up with 570. How interesting is that, he thought, both these numbers are also divisible by 570. But what had really astonished him was that the two founding personalities of these major religions, Jesus and Muhammad, were born exactly 570 years apart. Muhammad was born in 570 AD and Jesus, as far as the calendar was concerned, was born 0 AD!

Sebastian figured that since the end of the world date of 2280 AD was related to both the seven pairs and nineteen, he would multiply nineteen by seven. The answer was 133. He then added the total number of the seven pairs of numbers found on the slip of paper in the dark, musty room with broken furniture in Tucson. The numbers totaled 2147. 133+2147=2280.

"Wowie!", he exclaimed. *Ted would be proud of me,* he thought, with a hint of satisfaction, his lips curling into a slight smile.

Exposing the corruption around us, the greed that set the system in place, and our following it as a result of brainwashing would certainly bring the wasps out of the hive. But if the initial backlash could be controlled, there would be momentous implications. Knowing with certainty that not only did a Creator exist, but there was a willingness on the part of the Divine to communicate with us, to give us solutions to our problems and answers to our most pressing questions, would cause a huge shift in human behaviour.

Secularism as we know it would disappear completely. There would be a deep sense of awe, even shock in the minds of everyone. Even those who had believed in God would shiver that blind faith or belief had turned into the certainty of knowledge. The mere realization that there was a supernatural being watching over us, expecting actions from us and judging us would take us out of this trance we call materialism. Crime would be drastically reduced, almost to non-existent levels and a global effort would be undertaken to make a fresh start and to have a renewed relationship with God. All other issues would drift away into the background. Politicians, judges and other high-ranking officials would realize that there was added responsibility on their shoulders, a responsibility that if shirked they would be held accountable. As shocking as it seemed, we might even have honest government. With the truth coming out, people of different religions and nationalities would unite together in harmony. All this would happen based on intellectual acceptance of irrefutable evidence and solutions that benefited everyone. All this would happen in peace, not by war. This was not conjecture or a pipe dream. And it could all come true within a few years. According to Carl Sagan in his book *Contact*, the emergence of a mathematical code from outer space would "make everyone a believer."

Sebastian had to incorporate all this in his work. The seriousness of this also underscored the degree of political correctness and pandering to religious sensitivities that would be needed. To top all this, it would have to convey the same message when turned into a movie. Certainly seemed like a very tall order.

Sebastian had been busy preparing a plan on how to approach this. He had barely written for a week but made several notes in detail on how to promote the concepts of the script when the phone rang suddenly. He had been so busy, almost secluded in his office that he had not even realized he had a phone until he was startled by the ringing. It was Aunt Julie from San Diego. Sebastian was not very close to Aunt Julie. Yes, she was the only other surviving sister of his mother, but they had an on again, off again relationship.

With urgency in her voice she said, "Grace has had a major heart attack. She is in hospital here in San Diego, and you had better come right away. I don't know if she will pull through."

Off his feet at once, Sebastian collected some of his papers and stuffed them in his briefcase. Then he headed towards Jim's office. He was going to take a week off on personal grounds. He would promise to work from Aunt Julie's place so that he could meet his timeline.

Jim was quite agreeable to this. He knew Sebastian well even though he did not let up on that. His friend Jeremy Goldstein told him what a honest, dedicated and hard-working chap Sebastian was, and Jim had confidence in the young man's abilities.

* * * *

Three weeks had passed by and there was no word from Sebastian. Jim decided to go into his young story reviewer's office to try and find some contact information. He had deadlines to meet and a movie to produce. The studio needed to get moving because finances were starting to run low. Pinnacle had already gone through a round of layoffs earlier in the year and Jim did not want to lose more good people. He needed the existing employees to make the movie.

Jim entered Sebastian's office and sat at his desk. He began rummaging through the papers but could not find a contact name or number. There was a copy of the script and some scribbled notes spread over the desk. Was this not the script that had gotten Sebastian all excited and made him go abroad? Jim started reading this script.

The more he read the more alarmed Jim got. He began to understand the power of its content. But the implications of the script and the fact that there was proof of authenticity, something rare in religion, was unnerving. What worried him most was if this information became public. Even though he had told Sebastian to write it as fiction, it was still too potent. There was enough stuff here to bring down the whole system. It would create turmoil and insurmountable chaotic conditions in most critical institutions that had been considered noble. This script was suggesting a new economic, political and criminal justice system that was far superior to the existing ones, which would challenge the status quo of the present system. The world could not tolerate a society based on righteousness. There would be no wars and no arms industry. People would practice conservation of resources, move away from unproductive economic activity like drugs and the sex trade. International bankers, who controlled the economies and politics of nations, despite their excesses, provided stability and their enormous wealth was needed to bailout nations that struggled in the system they had created. True, they had done this in their own interest to amass personal fortunes, but there was merit in keeping the customer alive. A financially solvent customer is a repeat customer. If the customers drown or vanish, it is not good for business. You cannot squeeze blood from a turnip.

It also was a matter of personal interest for Jim. He knew how to play the system. He had gotten a lot of favours from people he knew in power, and if they disappeared it would be bad for the studio and bad for him.

The threats posed by these new ideas could simply not be allowed to materialize. It simply had to be stopped and stopped now before it got out of control. He thought of his friend the governor. The governor had to be notified immediately of this threat to national security, this threat to global institutions.

CHAPTER NINETEEN

SCRIPPS MERCY HOSPITAL IS A LARGE 433 BED hospital, a short distance away from the famed UC San Diego Medical Center. It is one of the top three hospitals in the San Diego area and ranked high on the list for adult procedures and patient safety. Sebastian turned off highway 163 onto West Washington Blvd and turned right into the hospital parking lot. He was anxious to see Gracie. His aunt was sixty-nine years old, and even though she was in good shape, a major heart attack would have been quite traumatic.

He hurried up to the fifth floor Cardiac unit and enquired at the nurses' desk. Gracie was in intensive care and out of consciousness. She had been given morphine to ease some of the pain and make her sleep. Sebastian could only see her from outside the glass window of the intensive care unit as she lay peacefully at rest. He decided he would return later when she might be awake. For the time being he wanted to find a place nearby where he could stay and work. He would also call Aunt Julie and meet with her later during the week.

Sebastian spent the afternoon scouting around the area for a place to stay. A block south of West Washington Blvd., on Robinson Street he found a vacancy in a modest red-bricked apartment building, the

Fireside Apartments. They were willing to accept monthly tenants, so he promptly signed up. Considering Gracie's condition he figured he would be staying here for a while.

It had been a week since he had really worked on his story, so he got down to it. Every day he would walk over to visit Gracie but would sadly come back because she was sleeping. Then he would continue working on his story. He planned the storyboard, made more notes and finally put pen to paper. At first it came slowly but then the words started flowing freely. Days turned into weeks and the month had already passed. He was so focussed that he did not even think of keeping Jim informed as to his whereabouts and status of the project. Now finally he had the finished product.

Across the street, on the rooftop of the Maritime Arms Hotel, Special Ops commander, William Botham, peered through his binoculars across the street towards the Fireside Apartments. He recalled the hectic events of the past forty-eight hours, starting with the urgent call on his secure line from the deputy CIA director. The director, as usual, only filled William in on the mission. William only knew it was a matter of extreme importance, a national security matter and that the target had to be eliminated. The CIA director had to locate Sebastian by his car plate number. After getting his address from Pinnacle's employee files, the CIA ran a match of the Department of Transportation database to find the plate number of the vehicle registered to a Sebastian Girard. Then with the special request for satellite surveillance, they had spotted this license plate from 100,000 feet above the parking lot of the Fireside Apartments in San Diego.

The special ops team had arrived there under cover of darkness the night before. Their Black Hawk helicopter landed in a nearby helipad, one of numerous across the country known only to a select few top field operations brass at the agency. The team were scuttled in a vehicle disguised as an ambulance and dropped off at the Scripps Mercy hospital less than a mile away, so as to not raise undue suspicions.

Now it was William's job to execute the plan. He had snipers covering the front and rear entrances to the building. The plan called for making sure that all copies of the story were found and destroyed. This meant not only checking the target's person but also his apartment. They did not want to kill him in the street. The idea was to shoot special bullets that would inject a substance into his bloodstream to make it look like he had a stroke or heart attack. Then one team would pick him up in an ambulance and drive him off to a secret location to interrogate him and find out where he had hidden copies of the story before terminating him. Another team would search his apartment for notes and other related items and seize his laptop computer.

Sebastian had rarely been outside except to visit Gracie, who lay in a comatose condition at Scripps Mercy. He had been working hard to complete his fictional account of the script and only taking limited breaks going downstairs to the sandwich shop and pharmacy, which were located on the ground floor of the Fireside Apartments. But today he was relieved, the story was finally done. He decided he was going to venture outside and treat himself to a fabulous lunch. He proceeded down the two flights of stairs from his third floor apartment and decided on the way to first stop at the pharmacy to pickup some postage stamps, a brown legal size envelope and a bottle of orange juice before he stepped out into what seemed to be a gorgeous, warm sunny day outside. He certainly had missed a lot of those in the last month.

Usually he was greeted with a familiar smile by the oriental owner of the pharmacy, but today John Ly had a nervous and worried look. He seemed quite distant, frequently glancing outside the window. Sebastian looked outside and realized that the normally busy street was very quiet.

Too quiet for this time of day, he thought. *Something does not seem right.*

After filling his shopping basket, he took his goods to John at the cash register.

"What's the matter John? Are you okay?"

"I am fine," replied John but his voice betrayed him.

"No, you are not. I can see it on your face. Come on, tell me, I want to help you." But John would not say anything. Instead he proceeded to ring the sales without as much as looking at Sebastian.

Just as Sebastian was about to exit the pharmacy and go outside, he heard a voice from behind "Wait," and turned around to see John beckon him back inside.

"Don't go out. There is danger. They have set the trap," he slowly said in a very serious voice.

Sebastian was taken aback. "What exactly do you mean? Who has set a trap and for whom?"

"I used to be a commando in the Vietnamese military back in 1970. See those people out there," he said, pointing outside the window. "They are special ops here for the kill. They are here to eliminate a target." Sebastian could see a couple of people across the street, one in a telephone booth, holding the receiver but looking towards the building every now and then. The other was smoking a cigarette and pretending to read the newspaper. "I spotted one field agent on the roof across the street, and if you look at the right most apartment, on the top floor across at the Maritime Arms Hotel, you will see through the drapes there is a M-16 rifle barrel sticking out, trained towards the entrance of this building."

At once Sebastian realized what had happened. In his hurry to meet Gracie, he had forgotten a copy of the script in his office. Because he had not contacted Jim, Jim must have entered his office and read the script. The script itself was too powerful to read, as he had experienced, and Jim must have been terrified as to what would happen if its contents were made public. Jim must have used his connections to try and stop the story he was writing. Jim certainly seemed to have connections at the highest levels. Jim had betrayed him!

Quickly he made his way up the stairs back to his apartment. He had to call Tina at once and tell her about Jim's betrayal and to get out of there. But when he called it was not Tina who picked up the phone. Sebastian felt his heart cringe when he heard the words "Tina does not work here anymore" as the person hung up the phone at the other end.

"Dear God, I hope she is okay," he said to himself.

There was no time to worry about Tina. Even though she was on his mind, this was a life and death situation and he had to act fast. Sebastian felt he could buy himself some time since the special ops would probably not come in and kill him unless they had no other alternative. Also they would make sure that they got all copies of the story. He could tone down his story, so it would not create turmoil. If there was any way to let Jim know that - but it was too late. Jim had already read the script. His only option was to send the story out, not to Pinnacle but to a competing studio in the hopes that they would consider making a movie. Once back in his apartment, he parted the curtains slightly and looked towards the gray stucco facade of the

Maritime Arms, turning his gaze towards the top floor of the right most apartment. He could see something glistening in the evening sunlight. John Ly was right. Just then he heard a flutter and a parrot landed on his window sill. The parrot had apparently flown from the blue US mail post box across the street to his window sill. There were two more parrots on the mail box. For some unexplained reason they were interested in making trips between the mail box and his window sill.

Sebastian had an idea. He would miniaturize the story, roll it up inside paper and put a stamp on it. Then he would put it around the parrot's leg. The parrot would carry it to the mailbox. There was a bus stop in front of the apartment's main entrance. He would catch the streetcar on his side of the street as soon as it stopped in front of the building, hoping that the streetcar would block the visibility of those across the street and in the building across. He would have to put on some kind of a disguise and act normal, yet do it with stealth so no one would realize it was him. Then he would disembark the streetcar three blocks down, find a mailbox and mail the brown paper envelope, returning via streetcar and observe the parrot to see if an opportunity presented itself to remove the rolled up paper parcel and put it in the mailbox. Seemed like a plan.

And it seemed to work perfectly. He first tried to reduce the story pages by making successive reductions at the photocopier in the pharmacy downstairs but after a few reductions, the clarity was totally lost. Then he tried with his 20 megapixel camera and had much better success. He printed the 3 x 6 inch result, rolled it in paper, affixed a stamp and slid it on the parrot's foot. The parrot flew away towards the mailbox and Sebastian headed to the front door of the hotel, with the stamped brown envelope containing the script tucked inside his jacket. He seized the right opportunity at the last minute to walk onto the streetcar as a bald, slightly bent over person with a limp.

It was not until he tried to get off the streetcar that the unexpected happened. He was hit by a speeding ambulance and fell to the ground. Luckily, he thought he suffered only minor bruises, but the paramedics insisted that there could be internal injuries and he should be transported to the hospital. Sebastian never got to the hospital. The last thing he remembered was being searched and interrogated, the sound of a gunshot and a piercing, excruciating pain in the centre of his chest. Suddenly he was overwhelmed by this strange turquoise light that seemed to stretch up into the heavens above and the last words he heard were, "Welcome into My servants. Welcome into My paradise." Somewhere in the distance a harp played a beautiful, soothing melody. And then everything blacked out.

CHAPTER TWENTY

WHEN HIS EYES OPENED, SEBASTIAN FOUND himself in the grandest of ballrooms. There must have been a few hundred people. He looked in awe as he admired the grandeur all around him. The ballroom had high ceilings, 30 feet high windows and beautiful paintings of animals, roses and portraits of happy people. Waiters were carrying golden trays filled with exotic fruits, pastries and appetizers. On both ends of the hall were massive tables laden with delicious meats of birds, seafood and juices of every flavour. There were wandering groups of musicians playing to the delight of the guests seated at tables. Other guests were dancing.

Sebastian realized he was dressed immaculately in a black tuxedo with a frilled white shirt and shiny shoes that felt like fur. As he walked past a few tables, looking around and absorbing the regalia, a couple suddenly stood up, called his name and started hugging him. To his utter bewilderment, it was Adrian and Betty.

"Son, we are so glad you could join us. We have been waiting for you. The ship is getting ready to leave for the final destination."

Sebastian felt he was in some sort of dream, and at first he felt awkward hugging the couple. Then he looked at their faces, which he had not seen until then because everything happened so suddenly. It was mom and dad! He found himself jumping up and down.

"Mummy! Daddy! I missed you so much. Please don't ever leave me again." They beckoned him to the empty seat beside them at a table. There was deep silence for a few minutes.

Finally when the shock wore off, he managed to utter, "Where are we going, again?"

"Son, let me show you," said Adrian as he stood up, held Sebastian's hand and walked over to the window. On the way Sebastian grabbed an avocado and shrimp sushi roll. Adrian pulled back the drapes. In front of them, about twenty miles in the distance, was a massive golden dome. From the centre of the dome, a strange turquoise light shone upwards towards the heavens. "We are going to the Eternity Meditation Chamber. It's much nicer in there."

Sebastian did not notice that behind the drapes, there were two smiling men who kept very silent. They were observing and did not wish to make themselves known. A gentle breeze was blowing in from the open window, and then Sebastian was almost knocked over as a winged creature suddenly swooshed down from nowhere, jerked the sushi roll from his hand and flew off. Sebastian could see it was a rather large bird, a hoopoe. As they turned around and walked back to the table, one of the men behind the drape whispered," I knew he would pass the test and make it, Michael."

"So, Dad, what are we waiting for," asked Sebastian.

"There are one or two people that they are still expecting, and then we leave." replied Adrian.

Just then, Gabriel Bollinger walked up to the PA system and announced, "Our last passengers have arrived. Ladies and Gentlemen, please get ready to board the red double-decker tour bus by the side entrance."

Then Sebastian saw her. This beautiful woman, looked like she was somewhere in her late thirties, it seemed. Gracie never looked more beautiful. Dressed in an elegant gold chiffon dress, she had large blue tanzanite earrings and a gold necklace with an emerald cube at its centre. She saw them and hurriedly walked towards Becky, her face beaming and sporting a lovely smile.

"My, my, look who we have here!" she exclaimed. "My dear sister and her husband". Then her eyes caught Sebastian's and she let out a squeal. "And my dear nephew."

They all got in line near the side entrance where the bus was. There were about one hundred and fifty people. Gracie was standing behind Sebastian. She had been relating to him how she would come in and out of consciousness at the hospital and then how she peacefully departed in a euphoric state during her sleep, as each angelic creature held her hand on either side and escorted her upward through some sort of energy beam. The line started moving, and as Sebastian turned around to face forward, he got a glimpse of red hair with a black head band and the unmistakable whiff of Dior J'adore. Before he realized what had happened, Tina Reeves had put her hands around his waist.

"Hello Sebastian," she whispered. "I missed you."

Sebastian's heart started racing once again. He simply said under his breath, "Omigod, I cannot believe what is happening." Tina started the conversation. "We have a lot to talk about, but let's wait until we have a few private moments together."

Upon boarding the bus they were all given complimentary cameras. Sebastian and Tina headed upstairs and towards the rear of the bus, so they could have some quiet.

Before Tina could begin, Sebastian anxiously asked, "What happened to your husband? You know I liked you and I got the impression that you liked me too, but you were wearing that wedding band on your finger, so I had to respect that."

Tina's answer almost made Sebastian jump out of his boots. "I only wore that to keep Jim off my back. He was trying to hit on me."

"What! Seriously?"

"Yes, and he still would not give up. Then one day he said he wanted to speak to me about a promotion and that we should talk over lunch. He took me out in this big car belonging to the studio manager to a deserted parking lot and made advances towards me. I tried to resist, but he overcame me. To hide his crime he then strangled me. It was horrible. I could feel his fingers tighten around my throat, and I desperately cried out for God to help me. Suddenly I felt like I was being lifted through an energy beam with beautiful harp music and the words "Welcome into My servants, welcome into My paradise." Before she knew it, she had found herself in the Grand Ballroom.

Sebastian took a few moments to digest all this. His body had started trembling.

After a minute of silence, they talked some more and Sebastian related his experiences of writing a script and being hunted down. He too heard the same words and harp music as he travelled through the energy beam upward to the Grand Ballroom.

They were so engrossed in their conversation that they hardly noticed the bus making its daily rounds through the streets of the Capital City, with a stop at the central square and its magnificent fountain. They did not hear Gabriel's announcement that it was a unique photo opportunity. As the bus wound itself further through the city streets, Sebastian looked at his watch. It was almost 7 pm. The bus rounded a corner and came to a stop. Ahead lay a drawbridge that was just coming down, so the bus could pass through.

A short while later they disembarked, stood in line and made their way up the steps to the meditation chamber. The giant doors swung open automatically as the first person in line neared it.

Sebastian thought, *Those massive steel doors must weigh at least twenty tons each. Yet they effortlessly opened without the slightest effort or sound. That's amazing.*

Once inside, Sebastian noticed opulence all around them. If Sebastian had thought that a meditation chamber would have austere surroundings he was very wrong. Instead, the Grand Ballroom was austere in comparison.

Each occupant of the Eternity Meditation Chamber was assigned to a mansion with surrounding gardens. There must have been a few hundred of these, Sebastian thought. There were streams and ponds. Through the middle of the chamber ran a river of milk and honey. Sebastian was so fascinated that he had hardly noticed Tina by his side, holding his hand. There were numerous handlers, aides and servers walking around helping the guests into their accommodations. Once inside, butlers and maids took care of the occupants every need.

Sebastian and Tina settled on luxurious green sofas and put on silk robes lined with gold laces that were handed to them. They sat back and sipped some delicious fruit nectar served from a translucent silver cup. It dawned on them that this meditation chamber was not to just sit and meditate but to remember the blessings bestowed upon them and give thanks. A voice seemed to be playing inside Sebastian's head "Your Lord has decreed the more you thank ME the more I will give you." He conferred with Tina and she confirmed that she was hearing the same words. It seemed like they were like the Kings and Queens on earth, even better off.

Tina did not want this to end. She had everything she wanted, health, wealth and happiness. Sebastian was there with her. But how long would this last and was this forever? She hoped so. She worried it might end, and too suddenly, that it was all a dream.

She beckoned one of the handlers.

"Excuse me, but do you know how long we will be here?" The handler spoke but she could not hear the words.

Instead, a little voice inside her head said, "You first have to strengthen your soul by being thankful in order to be ready for the next journey?"

"You mean there is still another journey," she said aloud but got no answer. "How will we know when we are ready?"

The voice inside her head spoke again.

"You will see a signal when the time is right."

* * * *

Cedric Johanson had been a widower for the last fifteen years. At the ripe old age of eighty-six he had lived a full life with a loving, faithful wife for over fifty years. His body was still in good shape because he walked a lot. There was one thing that was now the love of his life, his thirteen year old granddaughter in Germany, Alicia, who called him Grand Pops. He would make notes in his diary every day of events in his life, news and the stories that would interest her. Every Saturday morning he would walk out to the mailbox in front of the Fireside Apartments, about two blocks away, and mail a postcard to Alicia.

This Saturday morning seemed no different, except it was a bit windy and cool, as Cedric earnestly walked towards the mailbox, postcard in hand. He had just pushed the postcard into the mail slot when he heard a thud. Something fell on the mailbox from above, then landed onto the ground and bounced a few feet away. It was a small roll of paper covered with a postage stamp. He bent down and picked it up, turned it around and saw an address on it. This was very, very unusual.

"Maybe a love letter," he said jokingly as he put the roll into his coat pocket and went back home.

Once home, Cedric removed the roll from his coat pocket and looked at it more closely. He removed the paper cover and kept it aside. Then he unraveled the roll and saw very small writing. Using a magnifying glass that he kept in his bedside drawer for reading fine print in the newspaper, he saw that there were several pages of miniaturized writing. *What a clever idea. This person went to so much trouble. I really need to get this to the intended recipient.* An idea struck him, he would enlarge this and print it out on regular paper first and then mail it out in a brown paper envelope. He decided to go to the pharmacy in the Fireside Apartments. They had a photocopier that could print enlarged or reduced copies. Cedric figured that since the quality of the small print was so good, enlargement would still keep this quite legible.

* * * *

George Takimoto would receive about 50 stories a day. As story reviewer for Megafilm Studios, his job was to separate them into two piles. Pile A consisted of stories that were worth looking into. There were about one or two decent stories that came in every day. The rest were put in pile B, those destined to go into a dusty pile of rejected stories in the story archive room. As he went through the pile of incoming mail and stories, one story caught his attention. By habit, when he came across something that seemed interesting, he would turn to the last page to see the author and contact information. On this story, there was none. *An anonymous story? Who would do that? This must be some sort of prank. In any case I cannot do anything with it.* He tossed it into pile B. *This deserves to gather dust in the back. Perhaps in the future someone will make some sense of it.*

CHAPTER TWENTY ONE

"I KNOW WE ARE VERY COMFORTABLE HERE, BUT let's Go outside," Sebastian suggested to Tina. They wandered out, deciding to head in one direction to see how far they could go. Passing by many a magnificent estate on either side, laden with ponds, waterfalls and statues, and surrounded by flowers and trees, they were utterly impressed by the sheer size and grandeur hidden inside the domed structure. When they came to the end of the lane, they realized it was a dead end. What seemed to be a wall was actually a black epoxy coated surface giving a faint reflection.

Sebastian thought of how Jim had betrayed him and what he had done to Tina. He touched the interior of the meditation chamber wall. The surface came to life with bright pictures of Jim carrying out his evil deeds. His thoughts wandered to how his parents had died in a car accident and he found himself watching the accident unfold in front of him. Tina remembered her high school prom and vividly pictured herself as the homecoming queen in her pink satin dress with white embroidered lace. It was like they each had their own television screen that was finely tuned to their thoughts. At the bottom of the picture there was always this little red light, much like a traffic stop signal. Tina exclaimed, "Omigosh! That is the indicator. The handler said there would be a signal. When that light turns green, our soul will be ready to move on!"

With great apprehension, they withdrew from the wall and walked back towards their mansion.

For the next three days, the duo would meditate during the day on the wonders and blessings surrounding them and take a walk in the evening to the same dead end as they had before. On the third day they noticed the light at the bottom of their viewer had turned green.

"What do we do now?" Sebastian anxiously asked Tina.

"I don't know," she replied, "but let's head home. I am sure we can find a handler who will advise us."

As they made their way back along a deserted street, Sebastian noticed an old man with a pointed nose and a goatee, slightly hunched over walking towards them.

Excitedly, Sebastian ran over and exclaimed, "Papa?" The old man looked very surprised.

"My name is Zachariah Papadopoulos. How did you know they called me Papa? Only a few people are privy to that." Sebastian was at a loss of words to explain. This was deja vu. How was he to explain to this old man all that had happened, and that the old man had been a character in his fictional script.

He could only say, "You look like my grandfather."

Zack Papadopoulos replied, "Son, we are in the dimension of souls. The rules are all different here. We know many things here that we would not otherwise. Besides, I have several years of wisdom hidden behind this wrinkled face. I have served the good Lord for many, many years and now my time has come. I bet I look nothing like your grandfather, but I totally understand why you are saying that. You are both excited. You must have seen the green light. My light has turned green too. We must hasten at once to the glass enclosure in the middle of the Eternity Meditation Chamber."

The hesitation was gone. The trepidation was gone. They were all looking forward to the inevitable meeting with the source of all this creation. The walking turned brisk and soon they broke into a run. The street became very dark and lights appeared on the ground on either side of the road. It felt like they were on an airport runway with the lights directing them towards the glass enclosure that lay in the distance. The end of the journey seemed to be getting closer with every step they took.

Ahead a greenish blue light was leading them on. The road twisted and turned but the light stayed in front as a guide. The lighted road directed them down a paved staircase descending 300 feet into a dense jungle with rare animals and birds they had never seen or heard of before. Seemed like it was dusk and the lighted path abruptly ended. Now there were lights in the trees mapping out the path to take ahead of them. What really left an impression on Tina was how subdued the animals were, yet they seemed so content. Sebastian thought he may have spotted a grumpy lion with white paws that might be Ronaldo.

I wonder where Jake is. Probably busy stealing shrimp sushi in the Grand Ballroom, He chuckled. *Or on one more ride on the back of Bella.*

The jungle suddenly ended and the landscape opened up to a plateau with a beautiful sunset in the background. But what lay in the middle of the plateau stunned them. It was a beautiful glass enclosure about seven hundred feet high with what seemed like a miniature version of the northern lights dancing around above. The entire area was bathed in fascinating hues, pastel colours with enchanting music playing in the background. It seemed strange. Yet there was an euphoria of complete serenity.

As they approached the glass enclosure, they saw the blessed light was burning without any fuel from within the Emerald Basket. The light was so bright, reflecting between the concave mirrors, yet they did not have to shut their eyes or even squint. They just watched its beauty. When they were about five feet away, the light turned into a burning bush and they heard an authoritative, booming voice from within.

"I am the Lord, your God. The God of your father Abraham. Sebastian, I have made you just for me. That script was made under my watchful eye. Now you have come of age and fulfilled my plan. I can grant your every wish. Tell me what it is that you wish?"

Sebastian was shocked, flabbergasted and stumped all at once. He was standing there reverent and obedient without speaking a word. As a child he had watched the Ten Commandments. Now he felt like he was part of the movie, the part where Moses stands before the burning bush and talks to God atop Mount Sinai.

"Don't be shy, and don't be scared. You can tell me," the voice boomed

"Well, my Lord, I always was very fond of baseball. My hero was Babe Ruth. I would like to experience what it was to play like him, and hit all those home runs. Can I go back and relive . . ."

"You shall be Babe Ruth at the height of his career. And what about you Tina?"

Tina was shaking. She could barely utter a sound. It took a short while before the words barely came out.

"My fantasy is to be Cleopatra, the Queen of Egypt, romancing Julius Caesar"

"So it is spoken, so it shall be done," came the authoritative reply.

"My servant, Zachariah, and what would you like?"

Zachariah replied, "Most High, you know what I want. You are the knower of innermost thoughts."

The voice spoke, "But I want to hear it from you."

Zachariah continued, "My Lord, I just want to be your obedient servant like Abraham."

Sebastian smiled and thought he could have at least asked for a date with Melinda Watkins, recalling the sweet soft-spoken girl he had once liked.

"Adrian, Becky and your Aunt Grace were here a short while ago," the voice continued, "What I have planned for you is beyond your wildest imagination, beyond your most desirable fantasy. Are you ready to take a leap of faith?"

For a brief moment Sebastian hesitated as a thought came into his mind. What if either he or Tina did not make it to the other side? He had Tina, and they had a beautiful estate here, with servants catering to their every wish. He quickly dismissed the idea. Belief had carried him so far and faith was going to carry him the rest of the way.

The booming voice echoed again.

"I allowed the devil to tempt you one final time, and you passed the test. Now take the leap of faith."

Zachariah beckoned to the other two. "Let's hold hands and do it together."

"On the count of three," shouted Tina as they held hands

1-2-3

They all jumped together into the glass surface towards where the burning bush was. It had turned back into the Emerald Basket within the concave glass container from which emanated the blessed light.

The trio were engulfed in a sea of ecstasy. Senses were heightened and mental alacrity was at its maximum. It seemed like every cell in their body was screaming with joy. The pleasure was indescribable. As they sped upwards at millions of times the speed of light, through the window at the top of the dome, it felt like they were sailing on the wings of angels. The stars seemed to fall and fade away below them because of the enormous speed. It was like an express, custom space odyssey with a bird's eye view of the nebulas, the galaxies and the black holes. All these flashed by like passing lights.

They went through what seemed like seven black holes, gates through which they entered bigger universes, going higher and higher. There were great marvels in each universe, Sebastian recounted, until they reached the ultimate point.

Sebastian glanced back and could see the smallest universe the size of a golf ball.

"My gosh! I would need binoculars just to spot our Milky Way Galaxy," he said turning towards Tina.

They emerged from the outermost of the seven universes to a sight so magnificent, a splendour so overwhelming and breathtaking that it left them totally speechless. An infinite white plain field stretched from horizon to horizon in every direction with a majestic four-tiered throne of diamonds in the middle around which there were countless floating angels chanting what appeared to be the ultimate prayer.

"Praise be to God, Lord of the Universe."

Below them was a never ending blanket of fluffy white clouds. Through gaps in the clouds they could see the seven concentric universes and the earth. The earth was shining brightly from the light of its Creator. It had completed the task of providing food and shelter for its temporary inhabitants.

Deep within the bowels of the earth was an abysmal darkness. From the depths of the void the sneering, defiant voice of Luciano Vargas rang out into a sea of emptiness.

Above them the sky was dotted with crimson clouds. Each cloud was powered by its own sun and had a silver lining. A thousand moons reflected the light of a thousand suns and the entire area basked in a soft bluish white glow.

Around them, in every direction as far as the eye could see with their sharpened vision, stretched row upon row of creatures. Tina figured these were all the creatures that ever lived on the face of the earth. Seemed like there were countless billions. All were gathered in circular pattern facing the dazzling throne. It was an atmosphere of great reverence. Faces of those on the right seemed happy. Faces of those on the left seemed sad, and worried. Everyone stayed silent. Every head was bowed in the presence of the Almighty, the Most Gracious.

Sebastian remembered his GuTe luxury watch. It was unique. He remembered the salesman telling him at the time he purchased it that it showed not only the month and day but also had a feature to tell the year. Quickly he glanced at it and pushed the button on the side three times to reveal the year.

The year was 2280 AD. The human race was about to be judged.

EPILOGUE

THE CHILDREN WERE VERY CONCERNED. "sebastian and tina are missing. We fear some misfortune has befallen them."

Lawrence Forebearer could not bear to see the children redeyed and teary from crying. "I will go find them. I will go east and I will go west, and if I still do not find them, I will pursue yet another way," he promised.

After travelling far and wide, to the east and west, an exhaustive search produced no trace of Sebastian and Tina. Finally he decided to take the long route on horseback and embarked on a trek through the Great Steppe of Central Asia that stretches from eastern Europe to China. Following the same route taken by Alexander the Great some twenty-three centuries ago, he reached the valley of the Palisades and found himself standing in front of the legendary Iron Gates of Alexander, gates the conqueror had built to keep out the evil communities of Gog and Magog.

The massive iron gates he looked upon measured sixty feet high and about two hundred feet wide. They had been locked shut for ages and weighed several hundred tons. Lawrence Forebearer remembered the part of the story where the bravest made an undaunted sprint for the Pearly Gates where the ultimate prayer was being orchestrated. He disembarked from his white stallion and fell prostrate reciting the ultimate prayer three times. With a thunderous clamour and deafening grind, the Gates of Alexander started opening inward slowly.

Lawrence Forbearer walked a short distance to what appeared to be the centre of the village. There was a very strange sight to behold. In the middle of the square was a hexagonal glass-like structure about three stories high. Surrounding this were giant men, about twelve to thirteen feet tall. They were banging ceaselessly at the structure with their hammers, ice picks and other tools, even with their fists.

As he approached them, one of the giants said, "O wise one, we see that you have been endowed with many powers and bounties. Gog and Magog, at the behest of their leader Luciano Vargas have imprisoned these little people in a glass chamber. Can you help us rescue them please?"

The storyteller looked up and recognized Sebastian and Tina in the middle of an enormous crystal clear diamond. *My gosh! This must be worth more than all the gold in the world, and it is one of the hardest substances known to man.* He inspected the structure closely and found a hairline crack running from the centre to the surface.

"Bring me a stick," he said to one of the giants. "What kind of stick?" the giant replied

"One that is exactly two cubits long."

"But we have several that are two cubits long," the giant continued.

"It must be pointed at one end and have a handle at the other end."

"What kind of handle?" the giant asked.

Lawrence Forebearer was getting impatient. "The one with a golden handle."

"But we have more than one with a golden handle," the giant still insisted.

"The one that has never been used before."

Finally, the giant reluctantly conferred with some others and went to get the stick that Lawrence Forebearer requested.

Then he told the giants to move away from the diamond. He gently tapped the diamond at the exact spot of the flaw with the pointed end of the stick three times whereupon the entire diamond shattered and Sebastian and Tina fell to the ground.

The giants rushed to pick up the couple and played with them like toys. They carried them away to a little house they had built specially for them and tended to their every need.

"The story is now complete. I have no need for this anymore," said Lawrence Forbearer as he took out the trove of papers from his pocket on which the story was written, tore them into a thousand pieces and flung it into the dust. *I must go back for my work is done here. The children will be happy after all.*

"My dear Children. The time has come for me to tell you the real meaning behind the story. Sebastian and Tina represent Adam and Eve, the first humans sent down to earth with inspiration about the rebellion in heaven instigated by Satan. They are here to be tested with their faith like the rest of us; just as Satan is to be tested to prove his incompetence. Those who succumb to greed, lust and power will suffer and fail while those who uphold the virtues of hope, trust and goodness will ultimately be redeemed. This information is so important that I traveled to the ends of the world to deliver to the next generation who their most ardent foe is."

www.ingramcontent.com/pod-product-compliance
Ingram Content Group UK Ltd.
Pitfield, Milton Keynes, MK11 3LW, UK
UKHW042004230426
12048UKWH00009B/548